PINNED DOWN

The sniper was settled in a little pocket where he could command the valley. Crouching down against the rocks, Jim was not ten feet from this man. To achieve the pocket, however, there was a six-foot sheer of sand stone that he had to mount.

Gun in hand, he got his wind back, then swung himself up on the scarp. The man was lying on his belly, sighting his rifle. Jim's gun butt scraped loudly on the rock and the sniper whirled at the sound.

It was MaCumber. For one part of a second, he looked at Jim, and then he swiveled around, shooting wide from his hip in his haste for the mark. Jim, half his body over the edge, gun in hand, thumbed back the hammer, and MaCumber's body jogged abruptly. Surprise washed into his eyes. And then Jim, hanging there, emptied his gun at him.

SAVAGE RANGE

LUKE SHORT

A DELL BOOK

Published by
Dell Publishing
a division of
Bantam Doubleday Dell Publishing Group, Inc.
666 Fifth Avenue
New York, New York 10103

This story was first published in *Western Story Magazine* under the title "Trouble Fighter."

ISBN: 0-440-17963-7

Reprinted by arrangement with The Estate of Frederick D. Glidden

Printed in the United States of America

Published simultaneously in Canada

Four Previous Dell editions

December 1989

10 9 8 7 6 5 4 3 2 1

KRI

List of Chapters—

Savage Range

Chapter One: STRANGER FROM TEXAS

WHERE THE LONG PLATEAUS of New Mexico lift to join the towering march of the Rockies the clean length of Colorado, there is the town of San Jon, and Jim Wade, riding into it in a raw rain, thought it was the sorriest town he had ever looked upon. He was from Texas, too, used to little Spanish towns of rain-gutted adobe and sagging corrals of upended cedar poles.

But this town was different; it didn't follow any rules. To begin with, it lay on the west side of a wide and dry river, the Rio Puerco, and according to Jim Wade's judgment, the rivers in this high country should be narrow and wet. A sandy road, free of dripping underbrush, cut through the tall cottonwoods lining the river bottom, and then before the road properly pulled up off the bottom lands to a dry townsite, you were in San Jon.

Because a man likes things clear-cut, likes things either black or white and not gray, Jim Wade didn't like San Jon. It was neither American nor Spanish, but a sorry, wet jumble of the two. Along the wide and rutted road, which was always damp from the ground seep and was now pooled with dirty water, adobe houses squatted cheek by jowl with log shacks, and immediately, then, a man was in the plaza.

In the raw and whipping rain of late afternoon, the sight was disheartening. A freighting-outfit, ten teams and two tarp-hooded wagons in tandem, blocked out half the south side of the tiny plaza. The other three sides were a hodge-podge of frame, log, and adobe buildings, lighted against the early dusk.

The sight put Jim Wade in a truculent and restless frame of mind. His Levi's were soaking in spite of his slicker, for he had faced the rain all this day, and it was a cold rain, too soon off the Rockies to be warm and friendly.

Pulled up at one corner of the Plaza, he saw a man cut in front of him on the run for shelter across the street. Jim let him achieve the awninged walk and then pulled his horse over.

"Where'll I find shelter for my horse, *amigo*?" he asked in a soft Texas drawl.

The man paused, wheeled slowly in his tracks, and in that half-light appeared to be examining Jim. Then he said, "You can cut him up and wrap the chunks in your slicker for all I give a damn, mister," and went on down the walk.

There is a limit to a man's patience, and Jim Wade had reached his, although there was little about his long, tough-shaped face to indicate it. In a better light, a man might have taken warning from gray eyes, which were already smoldering a little from fourteen hours of discomfort.

He did not answer, only touched his pony's sides with his heels. Slowly, almost gracefully, Sleepy, his tired chestnut, stepped into motion, and Jim Wade reached down for his rope. He shook it out noiselessly, swiftly, built a big loop to allow for the darkness, and then, his eyes on the jogging back of the man on the sidewalk, made a swift, underhand cast beneath the wooden awning.

The whistle of the wet rope sounded a second's warning, so that the man half whirled when the loop settled around him. Then Sleepy sat on his haunches, backed up, and Jim Wade stepped out of the saddle. A good cutting horse never guessed, and Sleepy was a good cutting horse. He traveled slowly backward, keeping the rope taut, until the man's chest met the tie rail. Jim spoke softly, and Sleepy stopped, leaning a little of his magnificent weight backward to keep the rope taut and the man pinned.

Slowly, with an aching saddle stiffness, Jim Wade sloshed through the mud. Erect, he was a tall man, his slicker showing only his overwide flat shoulders and hiding the lean hips and the long, hard legs. He paused now in front of the man and cuffed his hat back off his forehead, revealing a shock of raven-black hair plastered to his forehead where the rain had crept up under his hatbrim.

"You couldn't be in a hurry, could you?" Jim asked.

The man made a violent move to grab for a gun holstered at his hip, but the rope cast had been expert, pinning his arms below the elbow. When he saw the futility of fighting it, he started to curse Jim in measured, level tones.

Jim smiled wolfishly and leaned his back against the tie rail. He didn't talk immediately, but brought out a cold pipe and placed it upside down in his mouth. The match he struck showed his face in bright and momentary relief, and it was an amused face, one primed for trouble and laughter and gaunted by long, hard rides.

"Down in Texas," he began, "we never ask questions, mister. That is, we never ask private questions that a man might resent. On the other hand, we can ask directions, the way to a drink, where we can find a bed—and where we can put up a horse. Now where was it you said I could find horse shelter? I'm some hard of hearin' in the rain."

"I dunno who you are," the man answered savagely, "but you better throw my gun out in the mud and get the hell out of here while you can!"

"Funny," Jim mused. "I can't make a thing out of them directions."

The man raised his head and bawled, "Ball! Miles!"

Idly, almost, Jim reached down, scooped up a handful of the thick adobe clay of the street, and plastered it in the man's mouth. His speech was shut off as abruptly as if cut with a knife. Carefully, Jim wiped his hand on his slicker while the man struggled to spit out the mud. It stayed.

Jim began again. "Now, a right smart hostler would locate a stable pretty close to the plaza, because that's where all his business centers. Reckon that buildin' over there on the southeast corner could be it?" He looked at his man. "If it is, you can nod your head yes."

He couldn't see the man's eyes, but he almost felt their savage glare. The man made a choking sound and then shook his head in negation.

Jim chuckled and shuttled his gaze along the row of buildings on the opposite side of the plaza. "Now that looks like a road comin' in from the northeast. Reckon it could be on that road?" Again he looked at the man, and this time the man mutely nodded in the affirmative.

"So?" Jim murmured. "That's what I thought to begin with, but I only aimed to make sure."

He reached down and pulled out the man's single gun. "I remember now. You wanted that gun throwed in the street, didn't you?" He threw it out into the mud and heard, but didn't see it splash in the pooled water. Then he spoke gently to Sleepy, who slacked off on the rope, and he slipped the noose over the man's shoulders.

The man's first act was to claw the mud out of his mouth, and Jim left him that way, spitting and coughing and swearing.

Halfway around the plaza, Jim heard his lifted voice, "You better ride, cowboy!"

For a few seconds, Jim was almost ashamed of himself, but it passed as he entered the long arch of the stable, located next to a corner of the plaza. A lantern had been put in the doorway, and an old man sat under it in a tilted-back chair, just out of the half circle of rain-swept planking.

He regarded Jim cautiously as he dismounted and off-saddled, and was close at hand when Jim said, "Feed him oats, old-timer. He's earned 'em."

The old man nodded and said tonelessly, "That'll be a dollar."

Jim grinned. "I'm not leavin' right away."

"You're a stranger, ain't you?"

"That's right."

"Then you pay now."

Jim scowled, regarding the old man with a puzzled suspicion. By long experience he knew that hostlers, as a class of men, are likely to be graveled by queer things, but he had never run up against such a demand as this.

"I don't get it," he drawled. "If I don't pay, you keep the horse. That's the way it runs, don't it?"

"Mebbe. Only you pay now." The old man looked bored, but it was a kindly boredom, and he almost smiled. "You see, this town ain't healthy for strangers, mister. Lots of 'em leaves a horse here and don't live to claim it. You" —he motioned briefly with his thumb to Jim—"being the new Excelsior foreman, I'd say your chances was even less than average. I'll take the dollar now, and you tell me who to send the money to when I sell your horse."

"So I'm the Excelsior foreman?" Jim asked. "Now, how do you know that? Nobody wrote it on the back of my slicker, did they?"

"No, but Bonsell made his brag."

"What brag?"

"He'd bring a man in here that would ram Excelsior down the throat of this country and make it stick. You look like you might be the man."

Jim's eyes narrowed slightly. "He did, did he? You mean he knew there was trouble comin' up?"

"Knew it!" The old man chuckled. "Hell, he's been here, ain't he? And he's got eyes, ain't he?" He surveyed Jim with a shrewdness that was not without kindliness.

"Never told you, then, when he seen you at Dodge?"

Jim shook his head faintly.

"Well, he said he caught you when you was broke, and that he had to put up a stake to get you out here. It's too late to turn back now." He put out a hand. "That'll be a dollar."

Jim handed him one and turned on his heel.

"One more thing," the old man called, and Jim paused. "I'd take off that slicker if I was you."

"Why?"

"It'll be like goin' into a gun fight with a woman's dress on."

Jim gazed speculatively at him, indecision in his face, and then he slowly unbuttoned his slicker and tied it on behind his saddle.

Tramping out the door and crossing the street in the rain, Jim Wade suddenly decided that he had more to learn about a company outfit than he expected. He was used to tough towns, almost expected them, but what the old hostler had told him disturbed him. He tried to remember what Bonsell had told him of his job when they met in Dodge, but the words wouldn't come. The gist of it was that the Excelsior outfit was taking over one of the old Spanish grants and they needed a man with cow savvy to set things right. And a man who has just lost a whole trail herd—twenty-five hundred head of prime Nueces longhorns—to Texas fever on the banks of the Cimarron, can't be very choosy where he works. It had sounded good to Jim Wade, and Jim Wade's reputation had sounded good to Max Bonsell. A fair exchange, money for experience. Only this sounded a bit different. He stopped under the wooden awning and, with the pelting of the rain above him, counted the days he had been on the trail. Yes, it came out exactly what Bonsell predicted. Therefore, since Bonsell said he'd meet him at the town's biggest saloon on the night of his arrival, the explanation wouldn't be far off.

He turned, then, satisfied, and set out to look for San Jon's biggest saloon.

Chapter Two: BATTLE IN THE MUD

IT WASN'T HARD TO FIND. Evidently the surly puncher Jim had argued with had been on his way to it, for it lay on the southwest corner of the plaza, and its doors, at the angle formed by the corner, let out clean shafts of light over the swing doors to turn the rain gray and thick and the street a wet wallow.

A scattering of ponies standing before it in the rain made Jim swear a little under his breath. The interior was typical, with a bar immediately to the left, and behind it the gambling-layouts. An ornate and heavy mirror backed the bar and reflected the glitter of row upon row of glasses, and beyond them the rough crowd. There were many men here, some prospectors, a few businessmen, one or two Mexican merchants in black broadcloth, the freighter, drunk as a lord, and the rest punchers and cattlemen.

Smoke was layered heavily under the overhead kerosene lamps at the gaming-tables, and a rough clatter of glasses and talk gave it the comfortable din of a social gathering.

Jim slipped in quietly and went immediately to the near end of the bar. "Where'll I find Max Bonsell?" he asked.

"Sittin' along one of the walls," the bartender said.

Walking slowly back toward the tables, Jim was aware that men were watching him in the bar mirror, and that there was no friendliness in their glances. Without a head being turned, he knew that word of his coming was traveling ahead of him up the room. He paused by the first table of poker and let his glance rove the room. Against the back wall, alone at a wall bench, Max Bonsell was seated over a drink. His wave attracted Jim's attention, and Jim crossed over to him. Sly and covert glances from the men at the gaming-tables did not escape him. It seemed that they were prepared for him, and it occurred to him that Max Bonsell might have appointed this saloon for a meeting-place so as to acquaint every man in the country with the new Excelsior foreman. It angered him a little, so that when he shook hands with Bonsell his greeting was a curt, "Howdy, Bonsell."

"Howdy, Jim. This is cutting the time as close as a man could ask for."

"Ain't it?" Jim murmured, and sat down.

The two of them made a sight that a man would look at twice. To a cowman it was obvious that they were both from Texas. It was in their speech, in their clothes, in their movements, in the shape of their faces. Only there was a difference. Max Bonsell had a length of leg that matched Jim's, only he was a little leaner, and there was something about his face that was inert and impassive and faintly wicked. His bleached eyes were cold and clear as mountain water, but a man couldn't look into them. It was as if a wall of arrogance were built behind them, so they were only surface-deep, guarding some quiet threat that lay in the man's mind. The skin of his face, oak-brown with lines ironed in it by the weather, was plastered close to his skull, and when he spoke tiny muscles flicked and sawed and reminded a man of a coiled spring. Jim's face, with that same long, bony shape, was more relaxed, gaunted only in the way a good race horse is gaunted. His gray eyes were slow and two miles deep, and he had a quick grin that would make a man stop cursing him and a woman feel all warm inside. He carried himself straighter, and if his look right now was be-damned-to-you, you felt it wasn't always that way.

He took the whisky Max Bonsell poured for him and downed it, then scoured his mouth with the back of his hand and said, "You didn't tell me at Dodge you were payin' fightin' wages."

"That's right, I didn't," Max Bonsell answered.

"Why?"

"Wanted to get you out here first."

"What if I don't take the job?"

Bonsell smiled meagerly at the room in general. "You got to live, don't you?"

"Not that way."

"What way?"

"I don't mind a fight when it's for somethin' I want," Jim murmured. "But other men's fights—no thanks."

"Somebody must have spooked you," Bonsell said after a pause.

"First man I talked to had sand in his craw, and the second one told me to pack a gun loose."

"That scare you?"

Jim's mouth tightened at the corners. "Quit it. I'm not a kid."

"All right. You got hired because I wanted a man that could handle a crew. I never knowed a Texan yet that didn't figure a scrap now and then was part of handlin' a crew."

Jim almost smiled. "Let's hear this setup before I promise anything."

Max Bonsell slipped out a sack of tobacco and rolled a smoke, and Jim packed his pipe and lighted it.

"Nothin' to tell except what I told you," Bonsell murmured. "My outfit, the Excelsior, has bought out this grant —the old Ulibarri grant. They picked it up for a lot of back taxes, and the title's clear. It's been fifteen years since an Ulibarri lived on it, and in that time a whole damn countryful of seven-cow outfits has moved in on its free grass. They got no right on it and they've never paid lease money. They treat it like open range. The first job Excelsior faces is runnin' them off. We warn them first, then push their beef off, and if it comes to trouble we fight for our property." He looked over lazily at Jim. "That sound like I lied to you?"

"Not much."

"Not any. I told you we was takin' over a Spanish grant. You've seen enough of that stuff to know what to expect."

"That's right," Jim agreed.

"I named a good wage—not a fightin' wage, exactly— because I figured you were a good man. You wouldn't run from a bluff and you wouldn't hunt trouble. And you knew cattle. If I'm wrong, tell me different."

Jim drawled, "And yet you got the whole country fightin' me to start with."

"That bother you? I've been sittin' here all evenin'."

"Had a drink with anybody?" Jim asked dryly, and he saw the flush creep into Bonsell's face.

Bonsell said, "No. They've got no love for Excelsior. But they're scared."

"They can get over that."

Bonsell shrugged and smoked, his eyes watchful and hard. He had had his say, Jim knew. If he wanted to shake hands with Bonsell now and walk out of here, get his horse, and ride off, there was nothing to stop him. But there was a kind of indirect flattery in what Max Bonsell said that made Jim hesitate. Max Bonsell needed a good man, one not wholly a fighter and one not wholly a cowman. The combination, outside of Texas, was hard to find, and Bonsell thought Jim Wade was the man. Again, with about three silver dollars to rattle in his pocket, what kind of a fool would he be to turn down this reasonable proposition? He'd fought to get his little spread down in Texas and he'd fought rustlers to keep it. He'd fought a crooked sheriff and a crooked county board. He'd fought trail rustlers and he'd fought other drovers on the Chisholm, and when he got to Dodge and Oglalla he'd fought Yankee marshals and Texas hardcases. He was sick of it, but that was no reason why a man had to hunt a hole, like a rabbit, and hide in it. The facts were plain enough and always had been; you fought your whole life long if you wanted to live.

He said briefly, "I'll take it. How many men—"

A commotion at one of the crowded faro tables beside him silenced him. A chair crashed over backward, and there was a sudden scuffling of feet. The hard, strident voice of the dealer rose over the clatter of the room, and it was cursing in bitter, spaced violence.

A man swung out from behind the bar, a man Jim had not noticed before. He was a mountain of a man, his bones smothered in great folds of flesh that caricatured every line of him. He lunged out into the clear, and Jim saw that his right leg was gone, the empty trouser leg pinned up. A thick oak crutch was propped under his arm, and he strangely contrived to move with an agility which was as swift as it was ponderous. He shouldered a loafer out of his way, sending him spinning, and then he plowed into the handful of men who had crowded around the quarrel. They parted for him, and he stopped under the lamp, his shaven head round and set stubbornly on his shoulders and beaded with a fine sweat.

He reached out and yanked a thick-bodied, bearded puncher up from the table and spun him against the wall. A slim, gangling young man whose back had been pinned on the table top rolled off and stumbled to his feet. A smear of red crossed his mouth, and he was breathing deeply.

"Keep out of this, Cope!" the puncher against the wall said mildly.

The heavy man swung ponderously on his crutch. "You take that row outside," he replied just as mildly.

The kid, hardly more than eighteen, scoured his bleeding

mouth with the back of his hand and glared beyond Cope at the puncher. It was this man the room watched, as if expecting him to give the cue. He was almost middle-aged, heavy in a way that was overmuscled, brutal. There was a kind of cheerful cruelty in his face that played in his eyes, his twisted, amused mouth behind his beard, and in his manner which held an exuberant arrogance. He rubbed the flat of his square palm across his beard and laughed. Then he hit Cope on the side of the head. It made a dull, solid, smacking noise. Cope's head did not move. He shook it a little, then lifted his crutch and brought it down at the stocky man, who dodged and missed it. Cope put the crutch under his arm again.

"Don't get me mad, Will-John," Cope said gently. "Take it outside like I said."

Will-John smiled lazily and looked over at the kid. "Sure," he murmured. "That kid had snaked six sleepers off me tonight. I'll put up with five. Not more, though."

He walked over to the kid and grabbed his shirt in his fist. The kid hit him in the face, and he laughed. The kid tried to stand his ground, but he couldn't. He was pushed down the barway by Will-John's lazy strength and then out the door into the rain. The curious crowd followed. Cope loafed down the room behind them and took his low seat behind the bar.

Jim murmured, "This Cope isn't a man to ask for help, is he?"

Bonsell smiled faintly and rose. "Come and meet him. If he likes a man, he's a friend."

Cope, still seated behind the bar, looked up at their approach and Bonsell said, "Cope, this is Jim Wade, the new boss at the Excelsior."

Cope's veiled eyes regarded Jim closely, and he put out a big hand which was not flabby. "Howdy," he said. He nodded toward the door. "Don't let that bother you, Wade.

My tables are square, and I serve all comers. But I won't allow a fight here and I won't take a side." He pulled up a bottle. "Have a drink."

Jim and Bonsell accepted the drink. It was strangely silent here in the saloon now, so that the silence outside was even more pronounced. Threading through it, barely audible, was the sound of muffled sobbing, nothing more.

Jim, curious, looked at Cope, a question in his eyes.

Cope said, "This Will-John can be pretty rough sometimes."

Jim set down his glass and strolled to the door. He shouldered through it and paused on the single step. The crowd, unmindful of the rain, lined the walk of the street that led to the plaza. The lamp in the lobby of the hotel across the street laid a dim light out on the shining mud of the street.

The kid was down in that mud, crawling. When he would fight to his knees, Will-John would stomp him down again. It was patient bullying; Will-John was absorbed by it.

He would stomp the kid into the mud and then he would raise his head to look across the street at someone in the shadow of the hotel.

"Here he is," Will-John called, his voice almost quiet in the silent rain. "I'll help him over. But he's got to crawl."

There was no answer from across the street, and Jim watched the kid drag himself to his knees, only to be stomped down by Will-John.

"He's a tinhorn, but he don't ring," Will-John observed, looking across the street again.

Jim felt that old feeling gathering inside him that might have been a warning if it didn't always come too late. He shouldered through the crowd, ducked under the tie rail, and walked through the sticky mud to Will-John.

"He's had enough," Jim said quietly.

Will-John did not turn at the sound of Jim's voice; he

didn't even look at him. He simply wheeled and hit out. Jim, almost surprised, chopped down on the blow, so that it hit him in the chest and sent him skidding back against the tie rail.

Will-John said, "I don't take Excelsior pay, mister, and I don't take Excelsior lip," and turned and stepped toward the kid.

Jim said quietly, "Turn around." Will-John lifted his leg to tromp the kid again. Jim's kick got in ahead of it. It sent Will-John ahead to trip over the kid and sprawl in the soupy mud.

He rolled over easily and rose and came toward Jim, fists at his side. "You got warned," he murmured, laughing a little. "Don't ever say you didn't."

His rush was swift, seemingly propelled by flailing arms. Jim hit out, beating down, so that his left arm hooked into Will-John's right and tangled, and then he rolled to the side, driving in his right arm and straightening it. He felt and heard the blow, which missed the shelving jaw and hit the neck. Almost gracefully, Will-John wheeled to the side, his head up now. Jim hit him in the face on the way down. Will-John sat there a moment, hands in the gummy adobe, and then he rose.

There was no speech this time. He set himself firmly in the mud, then leaned off balance forward, arms raised, and dug in his heels in a heavy, driving charge. Jim met it with his shoulder turned, and with his right hand he reached out and grabbed Will-John's hair and yanked his head back. With his left, he smashed down on Will-John's face three times before he released his grip and let him fall. This time he did not wait for Will-John to rise. He stood over him and, by balling up his shirt front and heaving, he lifted him to his knees. He knocked him down again and then stood there, breathing deeply, wet and furious.

"Get up," he said.

"I've had enough," Will-John mumbled. He pushed himself to his elbow, and then Jim lifted him to his feet again. He hit him twice and then caught him before he fell, and with a savage, rolling heave he threw him into the tie rail. It splintered and broke with a flat crack, and Will-John caromed into an onlooker. They both went down. The onlooker got up quickly, swearing, but Will-John lay there on his side on the wet sidewalk, face pillowed on his arm.

Jim raised his glance to scan the crowd, who eyed him silently.

"I don't like this town," he drawled quietly. "Anybody object to that?"

There was a faint stirring among the onlookers, and then they broke up. Jim stood there in the muddy road until they had either gone into the saloon or down the walk. He saw Cope then. Cope was standing on the step of his saloon, leaning lightly on his crutch. He looked down at Jim and then at Will-John and then said musingly, "You ain't the first man that thought that, Wade, but you're the first that said it," and went inside.

Something stirred behind Jim, and he turned. A woman had come out of the shadow across the street and was bent over the kid. She rolled him over and was feeling gingerly along his ribs.

"Where does he live?" Jim asked.

"I can do it," the woman said, not looking up.

Jim said, "Let me." Gently he pushed her aside and picked the soaked kid up in his arms. His body was slack, limp as thread.

They faced each other now in the rain, and Jim saw that this was a girl. Her slim, rather hungry-looking face was twisted into a sardonic smile, and as her glance touched Jim's face for a moment it was hostile, bitter. Then she gestured lazily down the street.

"I've done it enough," she said quietly and turned. "Come along, then."

She kept ahead of him. They passed down the side of the hotel, in front of a blacksmith shop where two men were shoeing a span of mules, and turned in on the other side of it.

It was a mean shack of logs set back from the road and abutting the frame blacksmith shop. The room he entered was low-ceilinged, clean, jammed with rickety furniture.

The girl indicated a sofa, whose plush was worn and blackened, and Jim said, "He's pretty wet. You better put a blanket over the sofa."

"Do you think it could look any worse?" the girl asked in a dead voice. "Put him down."

Jim did, asking, "Your brother?"

"Yes," she said wearily, indifferently. She disappeared through a door that was hung with an army blanket. Jim heard her pouring water into a basin, and presently she appeared with it and a towel and set to work on the kid. Beneath the hard and alert bitterness that shaped her face she was pretty. Her wet dress was of sun-faded blue calico. It was plain, clinging wetly to her and showing the slim full-breasted figure that somehow did not seem mature.

Jim's knuckles were smarting from mud ground into a cut, and he wrapped them in a handkerchief, watching her deft ministrations.

"What does he hold against you?" Jim asked suddenly.

The question startled her. When her face turned up to him, its reserve had dropped. "Will-John Cruver?"

"If that's his name, yes."

Her face veiled over, walling out his curiosity and any kindness he might have intended. Her glance dropped. "He wants me to live with him," she said quietly. She went on with her work, and then added, "He has a way of making people do what he wants. You'll find that out, maybe."

"I'll never see him again," Jim answered. "That's my hope."

"You're the new Excelsior foreman, aren't you?" she countered dryly. In explanation, she said, "He'll call the turn for Excelsior and he'll call it for you, too."

It was a plain statement, as if there was no room for doubt in her mind. Jim shifted his sogged boots, faintly irritated. Then Will-John Cruver must be one of the men whom Max Bonsell was trying to run off.

"You like the idea, maybe," Jim suggested meagerly.

Her head rose again, and there was a brash defiance in her eyes. "Yes. I don't like Will-John Cruver, but he's not a company man."

She turned back to her work. This time she felt the kid's ribs and then looked at the dirty bump on his temple again, where Cruver had clouted him.

Jim said thinly, "You need a dozen good meals and a new dress, maybe. Good night, miss."

He wheeled and went out into the rain, stooping low for the door. He heard her run after him, and he stopped and turned, regarding her as she stood framed in the doorway.

"I haven't forgotten all my manners," she said quietly. "Thank you for helping him."

"He's welcome," he said, and turned to go. He heard her walking after him, and he stopped again, and she came alongside him. The wet darkness seemed to lower the barrier of her hostility; she was so close to him that he could smell the warmth of her, and it made him impatient to be gone.

"Maybe you're right," she said in a low voice. "A dozen good meals and a new dress would make a difference." Her face tilted up to his. "There's only one way for a girl to live better than an army mule in this place, and I won't do that. But sometimes it's hard." She hesitated. "You're a kind man, I think. Maybe you understood my sharpness."

Jim stood motionless, trying to see her face. He reached for his cold pipe and put it in his mouth. "Your brother," he said. "Is he any good?"

"Not much. He's never had a chance to be."

"Has he ever worked cattle?"

"Yes. But his jobs never lasted."

"I'll need riders," Jim said in a matter-of-fact voice. "If he's any good, I'll pay him forty a month. Ten of that I'll send to you."

"I don't take charity!" she said sharply.

"That's the way it's got to be," Jim said brusquely and turned away.

He heard her quiet, resigned, "Thank you," and she went into the house.

Max Bonsell was waiting under the awning in front of the saloon. He tendered Jim his soaking hat and then drawled, "You sure get acquainted easy, Jim."

"Who was the kid?"

"Ben Beauchamp."

"And his sister? What's her name?"

"She's Tom Beauchamp's girl, Lily. He has the blacksmith shop."

They tramped silently down the walk, and then Jim said, "This Will-John Cruver, he claims to make pretty big tracks around here, eh?"

"About the biggest," Bonsell said dryly. "He heads that bunch of squatters."

Jim said nothing. They cut down the side of the plaza toward the stable. Jim said suddenly, "I wonder."

"What?"

"I had a sort of tangle with another *hombre* earlier in the evenin'. I wonder if he—"

"He was one of your own men," Bonsell said dryly, and let it go at that.

Chapter Three: MAN WITH A REPUTATION

HIS NAME, JIM FOUND OUT the following day, was Mel Ma-
Cumber, and he was a fair sample of the Excelsior crew.
After breakfast, served in the log cookshack, Jim went
back to the house for a dry pipe in his war bag, reflecting
on the strangeness of this outfit.

The crew had been quartered in two rooms of one of
the biggest houses Jim had ever seen. The main part was
adobe, two stories high with a white-railinged gallery
around all four sides. The wings, two of them, were of
square-hewn logs, and these had formerly held the ranch
office, a kitchen, a gun room, and storerooms. Mighty cottonwoods raised an arch over the house and shaded it, but
it was a magnificent old ghost of a house, nothing more.
The deep-set windows were paneless, and every third spoke
was missing from the gallery railing. Here and there a door
sagged off its hinges, and rank buffalo grass grew right up
to the house foundation of field stone. The old place was
dying, and the Excelsior, under Max Bonsell, had done little to revive it.

The two rooms of the lower story—where the Ulibarris
had entertained Governors General of Mexico, bishops,
and perfumed grandees from Castille visiting the colonies
—now echoed to the rough jests of a ranch crew, for this
was the bunkhouse. East, sloping toward the swift creek,
were the outbuildings, the cookshack, wagon sheds, barns,
the blacksmith shop, and the corrals. Beyond them was a
vast stretch of rolling country of wooded buttes and mesas,
where the dark green of big piñon and cedar shaded into
the lighter green of greasewood.

Jim found his pipe and came back to the door where he
packed and lighted it, his glance on the crew clustered in
front of the bunkhouse.

He had worked on enough spreads to know a fighting crew when he saw one, and a faint feeling of disgust welled up within him at sight of this one. Often enough such a crew was necessary, but he hated the idea of heading one. They were riffraff, composed partly of men on the dodge, out-and-out killers, and partly of men who would soon be on the dodge. They didn't like him, and he didn't like them, but there was never going to be any doubt in his mind as to who gave orders to the fifteen of them.

Having Bonsell's orders of last night in mind, Jim tramped down to the cookshack. They were gathered there, waiting for him, and fell silent at his approach. Ma-Cumber, slight and with an unhealthy pallor to his face, stood off a little way, eying Jim with shrewd, unblinking black eyes that distilled the poison for his glance.

"Ball," Jim said.

"Yeah?" This was an older man, grim-jawed and suspicious and quiet as death. Jim hoped his age had given him a little judgment.

"I'm givin' you the instructions, Ball. Miles, you and Pardee listen, because they're yours, too." His level eyes sought out the other two, and they nodded. "There's three spreads east of Mimbres Canyon. That's your territory, Ball. Miles, yours is west to the line and south as far as Wagon Butte. Pardee, yours is the rest of the lease. I want you three to ride to every spread in your territory. Tell them they've got till Sunday to get a man to me saying they're going to move. This is Tuesday. If they haven't a a man in here Sunday by midnight, we'll move against them. That's the warning and say it that way." He paused. "Also, you'll ride unarmed."

There was a moment's pause, and then someone said, "What the hell for?"

"Because you're told to," Jim answered quickly. "Any objections?"

"I ain't been without an iron since I was sixteen," Miles said surlily. "Send someone else."

"You'll ride out of here without a gun, or you'll ride out of here for good," Jim said. "What'll it be, Miles?"

Miles's glance slid over to Max Bonsell, who was smoking quietly a few paces away on the cookshack porch.

"How about it, Max?" Miles said.

"He's givin' you orders, I'm not," Max said quietly.

Miles looked back at Jim. "All right. Only what's the idea?"

"My idea of you, Miles," Jim murmured, "is that you can't talk without a gun to back you up. Well, you'd better start learnin'. As long as we're in the right here—and any court of law would bear us out—we'll go about this like white men, not Apaches. Those people deserve a warnin' and time to discuss it. Whatever they decide to do after that is on their own heads."

He paused, watching them.

"Another thing," he said slowly, his temper prodding him. "I haven't said this to Max Bonsell, but I'll say it to him now, in front of the whole crew. You take orders from me. There's no appeal to Bonsell. As far as you're concerned, there's one boss around here, and that's me." He looked over at Max. "That right?"

"That's right," Bonsell said.

Jim turned away. "As far as I'm concerned, the rest of you can light a shuck for town. Be back here by midnight Sunday, ready to ride."

They moved off toward the horse corral, and Jim walked over to Max.

"That's a prize collection of hardcases, Max. You must have cut sign on every outlaw hide-out between here and Pecos."

Max only grinned.

"I want a map of this lease," Jim announced. "Can you

draw me one, locatin' the spreads?"

Max could. They went inside the cookshack, and Bonsell sat down with pencil and paper. He was thus engaged when MaCumber appeared at the door.

"Gent to see you, Wade," he said.

"Who is it?"

"Sheriff."

Jim went out, Bonsell following, in time to see a man dismount from a claybank gelding and tie his reins to the grindstone in front of the cookshack.

Sheriff Link Haynes might have been fifty but he looked seventy. He had a narrow, suspicious face that was ravaged by dyspepsia and shaped by distrust. Of medium height, his comfortably sized paunch stemming from a flat chest seemed to pull him forward on his toes. His clothes were neat, clean, almost foppish, and the boots he wore on tiny feet were hand-tooled and beautiful.

"You Jim Wade?" he asked brusquely. You had a feeling he tried to make his voice deep and impressive, but he only succeeded in making it irritatingly harsh.

Jim nodded.

"I'm Sheriff Link Haynes." He made no move to extend his hand, so Jim only nodded coldly. He had a feeling he wasn't going to like this man. "Word's about in San Jon that when you blow in somethin' is goin' to happen."

Again Jim nodded.

"Well, it ain't," the sheriff announced flatly.

Jim's mouth started to turn up at the corners, and then a change came over his face. It became perfectly sober, respectful, but there were small dancing lights in his eyes.

"I wish I'd known that," Jim drawled, his voice rueful.

"What?"

"That a man like you was sheriff," Jim said. "They told me there was a rat-eaten old fool for sheriff here. Somebody lied to me."

"Who told you that?" the sheriff demanded hotly.

"A lady."

"A lady? Couldn't of been. Know her name?"

"Why, I thought she said it was Mrs. Link Haynes," Jim murmured. "Maybe I'm wrong."

Color crept into the sheriff's face, and he opened his mouth to speak, then shut it in a grim line. He glared at Jim's perfectly innocent face.

"I've heard about you," he announced. "They tell me you got a reputation in Dodge and the other trail towns for bein' the gent that always leads the hardcases in treein' the town. That right?"

Jim looked shyly at the sheriff and made a coy half circle with his boot sole in the dust. "I was young then, sir," he said modestly.

The yellow in the sheriff's face was flushed out by the red. He was about to get really angry.

"Let me tell you somethin', Wade," he said angrily. "This was a good country up till now. It'll be a damn sight better when you're out of it. And I aim to run you out."

Jim's tone changed immediately. "Do you, now?" he drawled.

"I do. First time you step over the line in any way, the first time I have a complaint agin you, you better ride. North or south, it don't matter which."

"Or you'll be chasin' me?" Jim murmured.

"I will."

Jim said quietly, "I heard you. Now you want a little advice?"

"No."

"You'll get some, anyway," Jim went on. "In the first place, my old pappy told me never to make a brag unless I could make it stick. You've made a brag that won't stick, Sheriff, because you or your ten twins couldn't run me out of this county. You couldn't run me out of anything, not even tobacco."

The sheriff just stared.

"In the second place," Jim went on, "I don't like the way you do business. Why, you're the very gent that brought me here."

"That's a lie!" Sheriff Haynes said.

"Think," Jim reminded him. "If you'd been any kind of a lawman at all, you'd know a few elementary laws you got to enforce. One of 'em is protection of private property. The Ulibarri grant is private property, but it's bein' trespassed on. The owners don't like it. If you was a decent sheriff with any sand in your craw, you'd run the squatters off. Instead of that, you try to run the owners off. Is that right?"

"They got here first!"

"Did they ever pay any lease money?"

"Nobody ever paid any lease money," Sheriff Haynes said emphatically. "Why, even when Mr. Buckner—he was the last of the Ulibarri blood that lived here—was here nobody paid any lease money. He never ranched, but he never gave a hang if other people did. This was open range then, and I aim to keep it so."

"It don't matter to you that it's been bought by this outfit?"

Link Haynes sneered. "Nobody but a renegade cowman likes a company outfit. They make a livin' by hoggin' range from honest men who need it!"

"And you'll help these—honest men?"

"As far as I can," Haynes said sturdily.

Jim nodded quietly. "It better not be very far, Sheriff. Because I sent notice of eviction to every man on this lease this mornin'."

"Servin' it with your gunmen, eh?"

Jim flushed a little this time. "Who I hire don't concern you, Haynes. I'm responsible for my crew, and they can be a bunch of Comanches for all you care."

"You're responsible, you say?"

"I said it, didn't I?"

Sheriff Haynes nodded wisely. "All right. That's one thing settled. That'll give me a handle to run you out of this county twice as fast as I would have anyway."

"You try it," Jim invited.

"I'll do that," Sheriff Haynes promised, and strode over to his horse.

Jim and Max Bonsell watched him ride off, not without a certain dignity, and then Jim turned to Max.

"Nice fair sheriff," he murmured. "Where'd they find him? Under a loose board?"

Max Bonsell only grinned. "Begin to see my reason for hirin' a hardcase crew?"

"Yeah," Jim said thoughtfully. "Maybe you're right, at that."

When Jim got his map, he went down to the corral for Sleepy. The sight of him, standing sleek and big and clean-limbed in that cool sunshine cheered Jim up a little. He whistled to him, and the big gelding came over. He spooked away from the bridle a couple of times, and Jim swore affectionately at him. This was a game they played daily, one which neither of them took seriously, but one which Jim considered was Sleepy's right as a loyal and dependable friend. Once the bridle was on, Sleepy looked around him in a haughty, questioning way that made Jim sympathize with him. He felt that way himself, just a little. This was a queer outfit, one that gave you no confidence and no pride in your work. But it was too late to back out now. To begin with, he'd given Bonsell his word, and he regretted it now. And then there was that matter of the sheriff. He had a way that went against a man's grain, and the stubborn streak in Jim was aroused at his boasting. Out of the pure contrariness which often guides a man in his decision, Jim had decided that he would stay here just to see if Sheriff Haynes could run him out.

He was aware, suddenly, that he was being watched, and he turned slowly to regard Lily Beauchamp's brother watching him from the top pole of the corral. Ben Beauchamp had a good face to begin with, fine-lined and clean-looking, but he wore an insufferable expression on it that irritated a man. Even the tow hair and the lithe, slim build of him couldn't change that.

Jim, remembering the quiet desperation of the girl, resolved to check his impulse. He said, "Mornin'."

"That ain't a bad horse," Ben Beauchamp observed, "but I've seen better."

"Where?"

Beauchamp was a little astonished at the bluntness of Jim's retort. "Right here," he said, holding up the reins in his hand. Jim walked over and looked at the big, Roman-nosed blue that Ben Beauchamp was riding.

"Can he run?" he asked mildly.

"Faster'n that chestnut."

"Want to bet?"

The kid looked appraisingly at the chestnut again. "Sure."

"My horse against yours."

"All right. Where do we race?"

Jim glanced over toward the creek. There was a flat, level stretch that paralleled it for six hundred yards or so to the timber gate toward the south. He said, "From even with the corral down to that far gate. It's open. First man through wins."

"Any dog holes there?"

"I'll see," Jim said. He mounted and rode out toward the creek. The inspection, which served to limber up Sleepy, revealed no prairie-dog holes, and Jim came back to the starting-line. Ben Beauchamp's face had fallen a little when he saw Sleepy canter, but he put back the sneer on his face when Jim approached.

"I dunno what I'll do with him when I win him," he announced to Jim.

Jim grinned secretly and said, "You give the word."

They lined up even, and at Ben Beauchamp's shout they started off. Sleepy, sensing a race but not quite sure of it, watched the blue shoot off like a skyrocket. Then he got it into his head what it was all about and stretched out. At the halfway mark, he pulled abreast of the blue, and it was then that Jim touched his heels to him. Sleepy was sure then. He settled lower, stretched longer, and was gone, and when they came to the gate he was leading by an easy thirty yards.

Jim pulled up and waited for Ben to come through the gate. He did, scowling. "Hit a dog hole," he growled. "Lucky I didn't break my neck."

"You don't think it was a fair race?"

"Oh, I'll stick by my word," Ben said.

"Give me that lane and we'll race back," Jim suggested.

Ben agreed and they changed sides. The race back was more uneven than the first. Sleepy was in one of his rare competitive moods, and then apparently decided to run just for the hell of it. He beat the blue by fifty yards this time.

When Ben rode up alongside Jim, he nodded and said, "He's better, all right." He paused, and Jim could see the reluctance in his manner. "Well, that leaves me afoot, don't it?"

"I reckon," Jim said.

"Loan me a horse, will you?"

"What for?"

"I'm headin' back for San Jon."

"Don't want the job?"

Ben looked around the place with a deliberate manner.

"I don't like the outfit so much."

"Well, so long," Jim said, reaching out for the blue's bridle.

Ben whipped around to regard Jim with surprise. He said, after a pause, "But I got to have a horse. Will you loan me one?"

"No."

Ben stared at him. "Why not?"

"Need 'em. Besides, you should have thought before you bet."

Anger flooded the kid's face, but he was shrewd, too. All his life he had been the kind of a kid who yelled names at the bigger kids then ducked in the house. It was still his instinct, and he carried it into barrooms or wherever he went. But the look on the face of this tall, gray-eyed Texan halted him. The memory of last night's beating was a little too fresh.

He said cautiously, "Suppose I take the job. Will you mount me?"

Jim nodded.

"All right. When do I start, then?"

Jim stifled a smile. "Right now. You're ridin' with me. We're makin' a five-day ride with ten pounds of jerky for grub." He pointed. "We head that way, toward the Star 88."

This was Ben Beauchamp's introduction to Jim Wade, and, if Jim was any judge, there would be something on that kid's face beside a sneer when they got home again.

To make doubly certain of this, he added, "And I'll take a bill of sale for that blue, too."

Chapter Four: CALL ME MASTER

A MAN CAN SEE a lot of country in five days, and the Uli-barri grant took in a lot of country. Roughly, it was eighty miles long, sixty miles wide, a grant dispensed by a Spanish king who had never seen it, but who hoped the gift of it would serve to keep one of his most bothersome courtiers across the sea.

By traveling fast and keeping to the ridges, Jim Wade and Ben Beauchamp saw a lot of it. It was an upended country rising to mountains in the north, but if there were rocky mesas, gaunt and boulder-strewn and serving only to make a man ride around them, there were also long sweeps of grassy valleys that ended in timber. It had taken its character from the weather, as all country does, so it was one of violent colors washed by driving rains, hard snows, and pushing winds. Nights, even in late spring, were cold, and it was no pleasure to stop just before dusk plunged into sheer dark, eat a dozen mouthfuls of jerky, and roll into cold blankets.

But Jim Wade was a thorough man, a general studying his battlefield. He came to understand why these squatters were reluctant to go. There were nine ranches on the lease, all of them a comfortable size, nestled snugly in some sheltered valley that cradled a hay field and full barns. It was well stocked with fat longhorns as wild and tough as the country.

The Star 88, closest to the mountains and farthest from San Jon, was the one he studied in particular. He saw it at sunrise, when the first thin streamer of smoke was lifting from the chimney of the log house. It was prosperous-looking, a working cattle ranch with nothing beautiful about it save the fat longhorns that grazed near it and the overstuffed barns and the sleek-looking horses in the corral.

The buildings themselves were backed into a tight rincon which, on three sides, scarcely left thirty yards of level ground before the sheer bulk of the mesa lifted up. It was Will-John Cruver's place, a large enough one to have a cookshack and bunkhouse. Of the five places Jim had seen, this was the biggest and most businesslike.

Jim's only distraction was Ben Beauchamp, and for the first two days it took all his patience to tolerate this kid. He was sulky, given to fits of talking and then long silences. But when he talked, he boasted, and when he boasted Jim only grinned and called him a piker. But he never got openly angry with the kid, and slowly it dawned upon Ben Beauchamp that this was a man who didn't care to hear of his deeds, good or bad, because he had done them all himself, and better. Ben began to take an interest in what they were doing about the fourth day. Then his weariness conquered, and he asked to go back to the Excelsior. Jim forbade, and further pointed out that if Ben left, he was technically riding a stolen horse, for which crime Jim would gladly prosecute him. To add to Ben's misery, they rode in rain all the last day, so that when they reached the Excelsior after dark Sunday night, he was wet and exhausted and famished and too weary to be surly.

Monday morning, Jim went first to Max Bonsell. No squatter had come in to acknowledge his error, so eviction was the next move.

After breakfast, Jim called the crew together. They were a shaky-looking lot, having spent most of their week in San Jon, drunk. Standing on the porch beside Max Bonsell, he wondered if all the ranchers had been warned. He had only the word of Miles, Ball, and Pardee. Ball, the most trustworthy, he was certain had done his task; but the other two he was doubtful of. However, Ball's ride had included the Star 88, which was what he wanted.

He counted off MaCumber, Ball, Miles, Ben Beauchamp, and a slim, quiet, bearded man named Scoville, and then said, "Saddle up."

"Where to?" MaCumber asked.

"Star 88. They won't move, so we move 'em."

The satisfaction in the faces of these men was plain, all except Ben Beauchamp. Resentment showed in his. The rest of the crew, Jim ordered, was to wait his return.

They were on the trail in twenty minutes but it was not the open-country riding that Excelsior riders wished for. They traveled across country, riding hard, clinging to the secret canyons and the brush and taking advantage of all the natural shelter.

When, after midday, Ball asked, "When do we noon, Wade?" Jim answered, "We don't."

Darkness caught them five miles or so from the Star 88, and under its protection, they traveled down in the valley. Jim seemed to know his way better than the others. When they came to the canyon in which lay the valley where the Star 88 was located, Jim took the first offshoot canyon to the west. They rode for another two hours, following its devious course until it had narrowed down to an arroyo scarcely wide enough for a horse.

Jim pulled up here and dismounted, and they rested in the dark, lighting smokes.

When the tobacco had taken the edge off their saddle weariness, Jim spoke.

"How many of you know the Star 88?"

All had seen it.

"Then this ought to be simple," Jim said. "MaCumber and Ball and Scoville take the north rim of that cup. Get as low down on it as you can without kicking off rock to give them warning. I'll take Beauchamp and Miles on the south side. You got that?"

They murmured assent.

"Now, get this straight," Jim said. "You're to get in your places and stay there. I'm goin' to fire that small hay barn for light. By the time it catches, I'll be up in the rocks on the south side. I'll strike a match when I get there. You strike one in answer to let me know you're set. Then I'll parley."

There was a silence, and MaCumber spoke up. "Parley? I thought this was a fight."

"Not your kind of a fight," Jim said quietly. "I'm goin' to warn Cruver and his crew off the place and then fire it. They'll go, I reckon. If they don't, I'll fire the shack. Now here's what I want understood. This is no killin' affair. If they hole up, you got a right to pour lead into that shack to scare 'em. But once it starts to burn, hold your fire. Let every man in that crew make a break for his horse and ride out. Once they start, you high-tail it for our horses. All I want is to clean that swarm of hornets out. And I don't want blood doin' it. Savvy that?"

There was a long silence, during which nobody spoke.

Jim said, menace in his tone, "The *hombre* that don't understand better speak out now. Because I mean it."

None answered, and Jim stood up. "All right. The place lies over this high ridge to the east. Scatter and find your holes."

He led the way with Ben and Miles, a feeling of uneasiness within him. There was a granite-hard and secret hatred of him among these men that stirred him to anger. They were a dare, just as an ugly bronc was a dare. While a man couldn't make an ugly bronc like him, he could make it respect him. There had never been a showdown between the Excelsior crew and himself, but there would be, he thought grimly.

His calculation had been right. They came out on the hogback directly at the house, and looking down and to the east he could see the close lights of the shack. The bunkhouse was dark, arguing that the crew was settled for the evening in Cruver's company.

Stealthily, Jim led the way down off the rim. It was steep, but the boulders were large and not easily dislodged.

When he was level with the end of the rincon, he indicated to Miles that he and Ben were to stay here. They were far above the roof of the house, perhaps seventy yards from it. Jim left his carbine and descended alone. He did not remember a dog about the place, so once on the level, he moved swiftly. Talk and laughter from the house drifted out into the chill air.

He passed the cookshack, walking carelessly and whistling, but the cook was in bed. He cut behind it to the small hay barn which, next to the cookshack, was the closest building to the house. It was a shed, rather, a roof on stilts sheltering a couple of tons of loose hay.

Swiftly, he pulled out handfuls of hay, trailing it on the ground to serve as a fuse. Then he lighted it, watched it flare up, and walked silently back to the talus of the mesa. By the time he had started to climb, the hay was afire. Its growing flame lighted the whole scene like a torch. Once in position beside Ben and Miles, he struck a match and, getting an answering flare from the opposite side of the rincon, he called loudly, "Cruver!"

For a second nothing happened, and then a man cautiously poked his head out the door. Catching sight of the fire, he turned and bawled back into the house.

Jim raised his gun and laid a shot across the doorstep. The lamp inside the house was extinguished immediately.

"Cruver!" he called. "Answer me!"

Silence, and then Cruver's full voice boomed out, "That's you, ain't it, Wade?"

Jim answered, "Clear out of this place, or we'll burn it on top of you!"

"What if we do?"

"Then walk to your horse corral and wait there till I tell you to go."

There was a long silence. Finally, surprisingly, Cruver yelled, "All right."

"Come ahead, then."

The first man tentatively stepped across the sill. Drawing no fire, he decided it was safe and started nonchalantly toward the corral. Suddenly, from the other side of the rincon, a shot whipped out, and the Star 88 hand stumbled, fell on his knees, and then rolled on his back.

Black fury mounted in Jim. He raised his rifle, sighted it at the spot where the gun flame showed, and fired. There was a wild yell in the night, and then Ball's voice bawled, "Cut it out!"

Jim yelled, "Hold your fire, damn you!"

Then he looked down at the shack again. The hit man had crawled back into the house.

"Cruver!"

"Go to hell, you bushwhacker!" Cruver yelled.

"Stay where you are if you don't want to get shot!" Jim called.

There was only one course left now. Cruver would not come out unless he was smoked out, since Jim had betrayed his word. And not one man in that shack would get out alive if those three across the rincon could help it. Still, angry reflection told Jim that the place would have to be burned unless Excelsior was to be laughed out of the country. And since Cruver had not put up a fight, Jim guessed that he had no guns in the house, but had left them in the bunkhouse. And that meant that Ball had not warned them.

Cursing bitterly, Jim slid down the mesa's talus again. His actions, plain as daylight, drew no fire from the house. First he let the horses out of the corral, then set about firing the place. With hay brought from the big barn, he set off the wagon shed, the big barn, the hay barn, the bunkhouse, and the cookshack.

A broken bale of hay he had saved out, and this he dragged back to the foot of the mesa. Calling Miles to help him, working like fury, he dragged the half bale up to where Ben Beauchamp, wide-eyed, was watching.

"Build a fire," he ordered then. "Light that hay and then roll it down against the blind end of that shack. Make it fast. If they try to come out, let 'em go. Only, if you hit one of 'em, I'll kill you!"

He vanished into the night then on a dead run, bound for the other side of the rincon. Halfway across it, he saw the hay start its fiery descent down the slope. Gathering speed, scattering a tail of sparks like a meteor, it bounded up in the air, leaping and bumping over rocks, hit the flat, and, carried by its momentum, rolled against the end of the shack. It settled there, almost burned out, and then the flames started to lick at the bark of the bottom row of logs.

The whole night was lighted now, so he had no trouble picking out Scoville, Ball, and MaCumber nestled behind a high rock halfway down the slope.

"Clear out!" Jim ordered from the rim.

Obediently they toiled back up the slope. By the time they reached the rim, Ben and Miles had come.

Jim waited until the three of them were erect, and then he asked calmly, "Who shot that man?"

There was no answer. MaCumber eyed him sullenly, even smiling a little. With a flick of his wrist, Jim palmed up his six-gun and said, "Ben, hear me?"

"Yes, sir," Ben said, his voice little and respectful now.

"Back off there fifteen yards, put a gun on this crew, and shoot the first man that tries to interfere."

He waited until Ben had done so. "Miles," Jim said. "Get over with the others."

Miles stepped over to join the other three. "Shuck your guns, boys," Jim drawled.

There was no mercy in his voice. Their guns dropped to the ground, and then he ordered them to step back.

"Now," he announced, "Which one of you coyotes shot that man?"

There was still no answer.

Jim threw his gun aside. "Step out here, Ball. You're biggest; I'll start with you."

"I never done it," Ball protested.

"Who did?"

No answer. Jim stepped over and slugged Ball in the face, knocking him back into Miles's arms. Ball straightened up, holding his mouth, but he did not want to fight. "MaCumber," he mumbled.

Jim's gaze shuttled to MaCumber, heavy and evil-looking in the glare of the burning buildings. "Well, well," he drawled. "That right, Scoville?"

"Yeah."

"Step out here," Jim murmured to MaCumber.

For answer, MaCumber stooped and picked up a rock. "Shall I let him have it?" Ben called.

"No," Jim answered. He advanced toward MaCumber. "There's some of you stuffed Stetsons around here that don't know your master," he drawled. "Watch and find out."

MaCumber said, "I'll beat your damn brains out if you come another step, Wade!"

Jim slugged out suddenly with his left, but it was a feint. MaCumber, deceived by it, brought the rock down, aiming for Jim's shoulder. Jim wheeled away and tripped him, and when the man fell, he was on him.

They never got off the ground again. MaCumber tried to hug Jim for protection, but, astraddle him, Jim slugged him in the body till he let go. Then Jim raised his aim and drove hard, sickening blows into MaCumber's face. He felt the man's nose flatten under his knuckles, and then he drove a fist into his mouth. Finally, MaCumber quit. He whined, bubbling blood from his cut lips, his eyes wild and terrified. When Jim stepped off him, Ma-Cumber sighed gently and started to sob, turning weakly on his face.

Jim looked up, his eyes still blazing. "Ball," he drawled between panting breaths, "I'm goin' to whittle you down, too."

But Ball wasn't fighting. Jim's first blow knocked him sprawling so that he teetered over the edge of the rock rim.

"Get up," Jim said.

"Not me," Ball said, making no move to rise. "I'm backin' water, Wade, and I don't care who knows it."

Jim wheeled to confront Miles and Scoville. "I'll take you two jokers on together," he offered, his voiced choked with fury.

Scoville raised a hand. "Not me, Wade. I know who cracks the whip around here."

"Get your guns," Jim taunted. "You're the kind of rats that don't feel like men without 'em. Get 'em, and we'll have a shoot-out now."

"You can lick me there, too," Scoville said mildly. "I wouldn't fight you for all the gold in Mexico, Wade. Now, cool down."

Jim stood there, panting deeply, and the color came back into his face. Ball scrambled to his feet, evading Jim's hot glance.

"Well, that's settled," Jim said quietly. "For money, marbles, or chalk, drunk or sober, day or night, with bricks, guns, fists, or bullwhips, I can lick the whole damn lot of you till you cry."

He glared around at them to see if they agreed, and apparently they did.

"All right, pick MaCumber up," Jim ordered and added, "you sorry damn bunch of tinhorn badmen."

MaCumber came to at the horses. He held on drunkenly while they rode off down the arroyo, and not a word was spoken the rest of that night.

Jim Wade had impressed his ability on five of these fifteen, and he had done more than that with Ben Beauchamp. For even a kid, behind any sneer he could wear, knew a man when he saw one. Ben Beauchamp was Jim Wade's man for life, and he wanted, strangely enough, to tell Jim that in all humbleness.

Chapter Five: "TILL HELL WON'T HAVE ME."

AT MIDNIGHT, when they rode into the Excelsior, saddle-weary and hungry, it was dark. Before they entered the gate, they were challenged by a sentry Max Bonsell had stationed, for this was likely to be war now.

Jim tumbled into his blankets amid the tired snores of the crew. Before breakfast, he hunted out Bonsell and told him what had happened, and Bonsell listened, his face impassive, as Jim related the fight and the reason for it.

"You're right," Bonsell said, when Jim finished. "Whip 'em into line." He flipped his cigarette away. "I reckon you better ride into San Jon today and see what the town says."

"Think that's wise?" Jim asked.

"You mean Haynes?" When Jim nodded, Max shrugged. "Suit yourself. Only my idea was to take the fight to him. If he thinks we're holin' up here afraid of him, he's liable to get wrong notions. Nobody's afraid of him, so what's the use of makin' him think we are? Of course"—he shrugged again—"you're runnin' this party. If you say no, then I'll forget it."

Jim frowned in thought. Obviously, the man MaCumber had shot was not badly hurt or he could not have crawled back to the shack. Since the burning was justified under the circumstances, there was a fighter's wisdom in what Bonsell had said.

"I'll do that," he murmured.

When the triangle clanged for breakfast and the crew assembled, they regarded Jim with a certain respect that had not been present before. Evidently the other ten men had been told by one of Jim's four that the ramrod was tough enough to make his orders stick.

After breakfast, Jim went down to the corral and saddled up. Ben Beauchamp followed him and, learning that he was riding to San Jon, asked if he could side him.

"Thinkin' of quittin'?" Jim asked.

Ben flushed and said immediately, "I'd stay here without wages, Jim."

"Then why do you want to go in?"

Ben mumbled something and then raised his glance to Jim's eyes and held it there and said, "I'd like to see Lily and tell her she'll see somethin' different from me now."

Jim nodded gravely and said, "Sure," feeling a pity for this kid who had found the only self-respect he had ever known among a bunch of riffraff hardcases. He felt ashamed of himself for permitting it, too.

The road to San Jon was an open one, but Jim rode cautiously, watching the country ahead of him. Will-John Cruver was not a man to wait for a break; he was the kind who would force one. It was rolling country, thick with piñons and cedar, but from the ridges a man could see the valley ahead of him.

It was on one of these ridges that Jim got a glimpse of some horsemen. He could not tell the number, but he picked out Sheriff Link Haynes's claybank. He smiled to himself and then said to Ben, "You let me handle this, Ben. You keep out of it."

They met at the bottom of the valley, where the trees were thick. Another man, probably a deputy, was with Sheriff Haynes. Haynes pulled up at sight of Jim and waited for him to approach. Jim stopped ten yards from him and regarded him with sardonic amusement. Haynes's face was a yellow color, as if his food was still troubling him.

"You ought to change cooks, Haynes," Jim drawled. "You look like you'd fried up a wagon bed and ate it without salt."

Haynes didn't answer immediately, and then he murmured, "Lord, and you can joke on this day."

"Why not?" Jim answered, grinning. "It was a fine one —until I saw you."

Haynes pursed his lips and whistled. Immediately there was a rustling in the brush. Jim wheeled his horse— too late. Five men, rifles to their shoulders, stepped out from behind him. When Jim looked around, Haynes and the deputy had a gun on him.

Jim said meagerly to Haynes, "I should never have trusted you this far, Sheriff."

One of the men behind Jim said, "Shall I let him have it, Link?"

"Bushwhackin'?" Jim inquired.

Haynes rode up to him and looked long in his face. There was an expression of disgust, almost horror, on Haynes's face that troubled Jim. The man wasn't angry, he was sick with loathing.

Jim looked about him at the others. They wore identical expressions.

"You gents must feel pretty strongly about your squatter friends," Jim observed.

The deputy raised his rifle, cursing. Haynes reached out and batted the gun aside just as it went off. But the deputy was furious.

"You low-down, scabby, murderin', bushwhackin' polecat," he said bitterly. "A man ought to lose his eyes, just for lookin' at you!"

Jim picked up one word from what the deputy had said, and his heart sank. "Did you say murderer?" he asked quietly.

They all looked at him and didn't speak.

"I saw that man shot," Jim said quietly. "I didn't think he was hurt bad."

Haynes opened his mouth to speak and then shut it again.

"Where did he die?" Jim asked.

"He?" Haynes asked. "There were thirteen 'he's' that died. Which one do you mean?"

Jim's eyes narrowed. "Thirteen? You mean there were thirteen men killed?"

Haynes said savagely, "You didn't know that, of course."

"Where?"

"Where your outfit killed 'em, damn you! Three at the Rocking L! Four at the Sliding H! Old man Benjamin at the Sundown! Two at the Chain Link! Three at the Bib K!"

"That's a lie!" Ben said hotly.

Jim raised a hand and said, "Quiet, Ben." To Haynes he said, "If those men were killed, they weren't killed by Excelsior!"

"Why, you lyin' tinhorn!" the deputy yelled. "They were seen! Old Lady Benjamin talked with Pardee. She heard him call to you. Lipscomb's kid at Bib K named five of your crew! He saw you on a chestnut."

Jim just stared at him, and then something went to pieces inside him. His face drained of color until it was gray, and slowly his glance fell to his hands on the horn. Those ten men he had left there at the house had waited for him to go, and then they had ridden out on their massacre. Not a single lease squatter had been warned of what to expect. Ball, Miles, and Pardee had never ridden out to warn them. The crew had waited until Jim was riding, until he would be seen by Cruver on his raid, and that same night they had struck. Without mercy, these killers had struck, and now no court in the land would believe that Jim Wade didn't head them.

He felt Haynes take his guns, and heard him say, "We better pull off the road, boys, if we want to dodge that lynch mob."

All day they kept to the brush, working toward San Jon. They were in sight of it by late afternoon, but they wanted the cover of darkness to smuggle Jim into the county jail. From what these grim-faced men dropped, it was evident that the whole countryside was in arms for Jim Wade, the foreman of this killer crew.

When darkness came and they were ready to ride, Jim said, "Haynes. I got a favor to ask of you."

"The only favor I'd do for you is shoot you," Haynes answered quietly. "And that would be a greater damn favor than you deserve."

"Turn this kid loose," Jim said quietly. "He's never taken a dollar of Excelsior pay. No man of all these squatters can claim they saw Ben Beauchamp."

Haynes hesitated, and Jim said urgently, "I'll take this on my own head. But don't drag an innocent kid into it."

Haynes said abruptly, "Beat it, Ben."

Ben Beauchamp sensed the temper of these men, and while he gladly would have gone against them, he understood there was some reason for Jim Wade wanting him free. Without a word, he mounted his blue and rode off.

The entry in town was quiet, by alleys, and on foot between houses until they entered the back door of the sheriff's office which was located on the corner of the plaza across from the hotel and catty-corner from Cope's Freighter's Pleasure saloon.

There was not a light in the sheriff's office, but as soon as Jim Wade entered it, he knew there were men in here.

It was thick with tobacco smoke, and he could make out the dim figures of men lounging against the wall.

When everyone was inside, Haynes said, "Bard, you here?"

"Yeah."

"Then get the preliminary hearing over pronto."

Jim couldn't see anyone, but he heard the solid tap of Cope's crutch as the heavy man moved in restlessness. The hearing was swift, with only legal questions asked.

Bard, apparently the justice of the peace, recited rapidly, "The prisoner, James Wade, is charged with the willful murder of thirteen persons, to wit—" and he droned out the names of the men killed by the Excelsior crew. "Does the prisoner plead guilty or not guilty to the charge?"

"Can I talk?" Jim asked.

"You haven't a lawyer. State your case."

Jim did. He had not planned the killings, he said with vehemence. He planned the raid on the Star 88. A man was shot, but not badly. As for the killings, they were planned by the crew, which got out of hand. He had no knowledge of the killings until Haynes told him, so help him God. His speech was met with silence.

Bard droned on. "Not guilty is the plea. You will be held for trial in the circuit court which convenes two weeks from this day. You are remanded to the custody of the sheriff."

"What about bail?" a weary voice asked.

"I will place the bail at two hundred thousand dollars," Bard answered, and this was met by grunts of satisfaction.

Someone approached him. It was Haynes, and he said, "Wade, I have deputized five men to guard this jail. They are five of the most honest men I know. My duty is to guard you until the date of your trial." He paused. "My sincere hope is that you are taken from my custody and killed. You deserve it. Now get into the cell block."

Alone in the single large cell, the window of which opened onto an alley running behind the building, Jim sank down on the cot and put his head in his hands. In the tomblike quiet of the cell, his thoughts began to take some order. Soon he began to perceive a pattern which underlay these events. The man behind it was, obviously, Max Bonsell. Bonsell had a job to do in driving off the squatters, a job which might take years of feuding. He preferred the quick way, the killer's way. But someone would have to pay for murder, even in this lawless country. He had gone to Dodge City in search of a man. That man had to have a reputation for handling men, a reputation as a gun fighter, and a reputation as an honest man. Jim Ward filled the bill and was hired. The rest was carefully planned, too. Jim Wade had had all the responsibility for the eviction of the squatters placed squarely on his shoulders. Moreover—and this was a stroke of blind fortune for Max Bonsell—Jim Wade had publicly and before the sheriff assumed that responsibility. All that remained was the raid. It had been planned nicely. While Jim, with a small crew, burned Cruver out, the others did the killing. In one swift stroke, most of the opposition to the Excelsior was wiped out. Instead of taking a year, it took a night.

But somebody had to answer for those murders—and Jim Wade was the man!

Bonsell could sanctimoniously claim that he knew nothing about it. Jim made a bet with himself that Bonsell had been in town the night before last, so his alibi would be perfect. As for the crew, they would vanish into the hills, leaving only Jim Wade, their foreman, to answer for them.

It was neat, merciless, complete.

Jim tried to look ahead. The chances were that when he was discovered in the jail, a lynch mob would form. And the length of his life after that depended on how ably those five men defended the jail.

And why should they defend it with their lives, knowing he was doomed, anyway?

He got up from the cot and started an examination of his cell. The jail was old, of adobe some three feet thick, with the five bars at the window sunk deep in the wall. Not an impossible jail to break out of in ordinary times, but impossible now, with five men quietly listening in the next room.

He was examining the ceiling when he heard a voice at the window.

"Jim Wade!" it whispered. "Jim Wade!"

Jim moved his cot over below the high window and stood on it. This brought his head level with the window, which was screened with heavy wire.

He looked into the slim, sad face of Lily Beauchamp.

"Lily!"

"Did they hurt you, Jim?"

"No."

"Oh, Jim, Ben told me about it! He knows you didn't do it because he was with you! What will happen?"

Jim whispered quietly, "Why, they'll either lynch or hang me if I don't get out of here."

"Can you?"

"It don't look like it," Jim confessed.

"But you've got to! And you've got to do it right away! The whole town is deserted, looking for you. But when word gets out you're captured, they'll come back and mob up!"

"Unh-hunh."

"Can you break out?"

"I'll try."

"Do you need tools?"

Jim smiled meagerly. "You'd have to cut the screen to get 'em to me and the racket would bring them in here."

Lily was silent a long while, and Jim was suddenly aware that she was sobbing.

"Lily, what's the matter?"

"I hate it! I hate it!" she whispered passionately.

Jim's face reflected surprise in that half-light.

Lily looked up at him and said, "Oh, I know it's strange, Jim, but can't you understand a girl? You—you're the first man who's ever treated me kindly, who hasn't asked for things I would never give. You're kind and—and you've done something for Ben. You've given me hope and—"

"You're excited, Lily," Jim said gravely. "Any man who wasn't blind could see how decent you are. If—well, if I don't come through this, don't get bitter and hard about it, girl. Watch Ben and make somethin' out of him. He's got the stuff."

"Jim," Lily whispered. "I love you. Is that—is that queer?"

Jim didn't answer.

"I've only seen you ten minutes in my whole life, but you've never been out of my mind since that night. Never!" She looked up and smiled. "I just wanted you to know. It doesn't make any difference to you, I know, because you don't love me. Only—only—good-by. And I'll get you out! I *will*, Jim!"

And she was gone. Jim stood there, looking out into the night, letting Lily Beauchamp's words sink into his mind. He felt small and humble before this girl, who had been honest enough to pour out her heart to him. Suddenly he gripped the bars until his knuckles were white. What the hell kind of a world was it that would beat and cow a girl like Lily into being so grateful for one decent act a man did for her? Cow her until she was so grateful for this act that she mistook her gratitude for love. For Jim Wade did not think for one instant that Lily Beauchamp loved him.

It was gratitude, gratitude for a kindness that any white man would have been glad to do.

He stood there watching the night. The dark form of a freight wagon on the street was the only thing he could clearly see. He'd better take a good look, he thought, because that freight wagon was the last thing he'd see when he was at peace with the world.

He climbed down and continued his examination of the cell. It was solid and had probably housed many men as desperate as he was until the hour of their sentence.

Lying down on the cot, he rehearsed all the jail escapes he had ever heard of. But all of them precluded a situation that was not guarded by five grim men in the next room.

He lay awake for hours, waiting for dawn, listening to the quiet of the town. If he ever got out of here, he would spend the rest of his life hunting down Max Bonsell and killing him. It was a wholly impersonal anger that did not include self-pity; it was an anger at injustice, at a frame-up.

A sound drifted into his consciousness and roused him. He listened. A sifting of gravel rattled faintly on the screen. Rising, he stood on the cot and looked out of the window. There was no one there. Then, just as he was about to step down off the cot, Cope's egg-bald head appeared.

"Well, you done it," Cope announced grimly.

Jim said guardedly, "Done what?" because hadn't he heard Cope out in the front room with those others?

"Didn't you suspect a damn thing about Bonsell?" Cope said angrily. "How old are you, Wade?"

"A broke man can't afford to suspect," Jim retorted.

"He can't afford not to," Cope replied. He was silent a minute. "Can you get out of there?"

"How?"

"I'm askin' you."

"Not without a gun."

"That's out." He paused. "I can get you out."

Jim hesitated. "Why should you?" he murmured.

"You're too good a bucko to die on a cottonwood limb, for one thing," Cope said gravely. "Another is, we need you."

"Who's 'we'?"

"Do you want out of there bad enough to find out?"

"I want out mighty bad," Jim said fervently.

"You aim to run when you're out?"

"Not before I nail Bonsell's hide to the wall," Jim answered quietly.

Cope almost chuckled. "Then you'll stick?"

"Till hell won't have me," Jim said.

"All right." With incredible silence, Cope hoisted a huge logging-chain up even with the window. He slipped its big hook between the bars and the screen, then hooked it over the shank of the chain.

"See that freight wagon?" Cope asked.

"Yes."

"In half an hour, Jody Capper will hook five teams to it and head for the mines at Tres Piedras. Those broncs will be salty and they'll try to break harness the minute they hear his whip. This chain will be hooked to the rear axle of the wagon. When the window goes out you follow it. Cut across behind the hotel, then turn right, and make for behind my saloon. There's stairs on the north side of it. Climb 'em and go into my rooms. I'll be there."

Jim was silent a long moment. "How do I know this isn't an excuse to avoid a trial by cuttin' down on me the minute I get out?"

"You don't," Cope said, and vanished from sight.

Jim watched. He saw Cope couple another length of logging-chain to the one at the window, then trail it over to the wagon. A third length he coupled to this, then, crawling under the wagon, he fastened it to the axle.

What he did next fascinated Jim. He moved leaves from the ditch over onto the logging-chain. When he came to the boardwalk, he lifted a section of it out from under the chain and put the walk back on top of it. Then, taking a whiskbroom from his hip pocket, he carefully brushed out his tracks, working especially hard on the indentations his crutch had made. When he was finished, he waved to Jim and vanished into the night.

The wait was interminable, but Jim never left the window. Later, much later, a light appeared in the shack next to the hotel. That would be Jody Capper breakfasting. Presently two men with a lantern emerged and went to the big barn fronting on the road. There was considerable swearing from within the barn and a long wait. Then the doors opened, and a pair of skittish broncs were led out by the man with the lantern. They were harnessed to the wheel place, and immediately another team was brought out. This went on until five teams, restive in the chill morning air, were harnessed to the wagon.

Jim almost choked once when the shortest man walked around behind the wagon and climbed the end gate to examine something inside. But he didn't touch the chain, and Jim breathed more freely again. The other man stood holding the bridle of the lead team, while the first one stood on the wagon bed, holding the reins and cursing the team. They started once, but the two men fought them so that they backed up beyond the former mark.

Then the man in the wagon, Jody Capper, Jim guessed, picked up a whip with his free hand and unleashed it. With a shout to the man holding the horses to clear out, he cracked his whip like a pistol shot.

The five half-broken teams exploded into their collars.

There was a long second when nothing happened, and then the chain sung taut, throwing the boardwalk high into the air.

A clang of screeching iron lifted into the night, and simultaneously, the rear end of the wagon lifted off the ground, and the whole window frame of the cell pulled out in a moil of dust.

Jim lunged through the opening in one jump, noting that the team was still on the run. Jody Capper was looking back, cursing in a wild voice, but it was not Jody Jim was watching. It was the man with the lantern, who had turned and was staring at him.

Jim hit him running, hit him hard enough to knock him sprawling, the lantern sailing through the air to smash in the road.

Scarcely pausing in his stride, he made for the alley behind the hotel. Rounding its rear corner, he heard the first yell from the jail.

When he crossed the street, it was at a walk, soundlessly. They could not see him, but they might hear him. Achieving the alley behind the saloon, he sped down it and found the stairs at the far side of it.

He climbed them slowly, silently, and opened the door facing the top platform. Immediately he stepped into a room burning one lamp and that only dimly.

Cope was mountainous in the middle of the room, his face grave and sweating.

Beside him stood the most beautiful woman Jim Wade had ever seen. She was dressed in a suit of dark-blue wool with a full, sweeping skirt. It sheered off at her neck, showing the fine sweep of her head which was crowned with a mass of corn-colored hair. Her face was surprised, so that her full lips were parted a little, and the excitement brought color to her cheeks. It was her eyes, bright with excitement and curiosity that Jim Wade looked at. They were deep-set behind low cheekbones, and dark as night pools.

"This is the man?" she murmured, in a full, low voice.

Cope grinned. "Good boy! Mary, this is Jim Wade. Jim, this is Mary Buckner, the real owner, the heir of the Ulibarri grant."

Without waiting for Mary to extend her hand, Cope blew out the light and said, "Go into that room."

Mary went in ahead of him, for Jim could smell her perfume. Cope closed the door on them, and they were in darkness.

Within fifteen seconds, there was a pounding on the stairs, and Jim heard a thundering knock at the door. Someone shouted, "Cope! Cope!"

Jim heard Cope mumble, "Yeah?" then a pause, and then the tap, tap of his crutch as he went to the door.

"He's gone!" a man said excitedly. "He broke jail!"

"Hell!" Cope exploded. "Get out of the way and let me see!"

They left, for the door slammed solidly.

Mary Buckner said quietly in the darkness, "We could go into the other room."

Chapter Six: STOLEN RANGE

THE LAMP WAS BURNING just as Cope left it when, supposedly, he was roused from bed.

By its light Jim Wade looked at Mary Buckner, and Mary Buckner looked at him. It was a friendly scrutiny from both of them, and at last Jim Wade grinned.

"This is comin' a little too fast for me. I—I don't know what to say."

"We might shake hands," Mary Buckner said gravely. "We're going to be friends, aren't we?"

They shook hands solemnly, and then Mary laughed. "Sit down."

Jim waited for her to take her chair, and then he sank onto the sofa.

"Cope told me everything that's happened," she began. "He's a loyal friend."

Jim smiled. "But I didn't even know he was one. To me, I mean."

"He's sharp. He can tell a crook a mile off—and he can like a man as quickly, too."

"But why—" Jim began, and stopped. Where to begin? He started off on another tack. "Did he say your name was Mary Buckner, ma'am?"

She nodded. "You've heard of us, I suppose?"

Jim nodded. "Barely. You are the family the Excelsior bought from?"

"Bought from?" Mary shook her head. "Hardly. I'm the one they stole it from."

She saw the puzzled expression on Jim's face, and she smiled. "Hadn't we better start from the beginning?"

"If there is one," Jim said fervently. "I landed in the middle of it. That's all I know."

She began to talk, and Jim found it hard to concentrate on her words. She was like something shining and clear that a man couldn't stare at enough. But he listened and he heard a strange story.

The Ulibarris, Mary Buckner said, were the original grantees, and the Buckners' claim to it was through one Simon Buckner, a Yankee ship's captain. His ship was wrecked on the west coast of Mexico in the late seventeen hundreds, after which he made his way to Mexico City. There he courted the only daughter of the Ulibarri house, Principia by name, and later eloped with her, taking her to Salem. When, after the Mexican War, title to this country was transferred to the U.S., it was found one Leonidas Buckner, Boston merchant, was heir to the Ulibarri grant. He had two sons, Harvey and James. Harvey was a scapegrace, James a semi-invalid. On the father's death, the Ulibarri property went to son James, who moved West with his daughter. That was James Buckner, and Mary was his daughter.

Soon after James Buckner moved into the old house, built by the Ulibarris long ago, the cattle business began to thrive. A rough type of cattleman began to encroach on the grant, and Will-John Cruver was one of them. James Buckner didn't mind; he wasn't a cattleman. But when the big estate began to drain away James Buckner's slim resources, he decided to run cattle. That had been the death of him.

"How do you mean, the death of him?" Jim asked.

"He ordered Cruver and the other squatters to leave," Mary said. "Rather than do it, they came to the house one night and shot him and took his body with them."

"You saw it?"

Mary only nodded quietly. "I was a little girl, and nobody would believe my story. I was left an orphan by that murder. I was ten years old then."

"How did you live?"

Mary's face softened a little. "I wouldn't have if it hadn't been for rough Jack Cope. His wife was alive then, and they adopted me. Later, when I was school age, Uncle Jack sent me to school in the East. When I was out of school, I was aching to come back to the West. I did come back—but to Wyoming as a schoolteacher."

"But your land," Jim said. "It's still yours?"

Mary shook her head. "It would take money to prove that in court, years of litigation. And I was poor."

"So you tried to save money for the court fight?"

Mary nodded. "That's just what I did." She leaned forward toward Jim. "You see, there were thousands of dollars in back taxes that I couldn't meet, so what was the sense of trying to win title? But I had one thing that gave me confidence."

"Jack Cope?"

Mary smiled and nodded. "Two things, then. Jack Cope was one. The other was the original charter from the King of Spain, given to Don Justino Perez y Santiago y Mudarra y Ulibarri. I had it in the bottom of my trunk." She laughed. "That was my war chest."

"You still have it, then?"

Mary shook her head slightly and leaned back in her chair. "It was stolen."

"Who did that?"

"My uncle, Harvey Buckner, I believe."

She told Jim then what he most wanted to know, explaining Max Bonsell's presence here. Harvey Buckner, so Jack Cope had told Mary, sent a man to San Jon after his brother's death. This man asked a lot of questions and drank a lot of whisky.

And his questions all pointed toward one thing. Had anybody seen James Buckner dead? Nobody had, except his girl, Mary, and she was gone somewhere these ten years back. Were they sure James Buckner was dead? No, nobody was, except the murderers—if he was murdered. And they doubted that. Months later the charter was stolen from Mary's trunk where she was staying in a little Wyoming cow town.

"But what does it get him?" Jim asked quickly.

"It makes him James Buckner," Mary answered simply. "For eight years he has lived in Santa Fe under the name of James Buckner. He looks enough like Dad that any witness would be hard put to tell the difference. He has established that name in this country far more strongly than Dad did. He has the original charter from the Spanish king. Under James Buckner's name, he has paid enough on the taxes of the old grant that it can't be sold for taxes. And now, in partnership with Max Bonsell, he is taking over."

Jim whistled in exclamation. "And the only men who

were soft with gratitude.

She turned away from him and walked into the bedroom. Jim, embarrassed and puzzled, packed his pipe now and lighted it.

Soon Mary came out and she said cheerfully, "It's daylight already, and I'm hungry. Are you?"

They cooked a breakfast in Jack Cope's tiny kitchen. His quarters were three small rooms above the rear end of his saloon, a kitchen, a bedroom, and a living-room. The furniture was sparse, masculine, and the rooms were as spruce and clean as the cabins of a crack China tea clipper.

Halfway through breakfast, they heard someone ascending the stairs. Jim listened tensely until he made out the thump of Jack Cope's crutch.

When Cope came in, Mary ran to him and threw her arms around his big shoulders and hugged him. "Uncle Jack, he'll help us! He promised!" she cried.

Cope's tough and muscled face didn't change. "I knew he would," he said shortly. "I've waited too long to make a mistake."

At breakfast, he told them what had happened. Sheriff Haynes was insane with fury. He had roused every ablebodied man in town. Cope suggested to him that they search the town, since there was no evidence that Jim Wade had ridden out.

"You suggested it, you say?" Mary said, laughing. "Aren't you afraid he'll do it?"

"He is doin' it."

"But—what about this place?"

"I'm safe enough," Cope growled. "You see it was my suggestion. It was also my suggestion that he go out and get Jim Wade before a wild-eyed posse could be organized. It was also my suggestion that the preliminary hearin' be held in the dark office and that Haynes deputize five of us to hold the jail."

"But how can you do it?" Mary asked.

Cope looked over at her, and his tough old face relaxed a little. He put a big hand on hers and said, "Mary, nobody knows it, but I run this town. I've spent fifteen years makin' my name respected, so when this time came no man would doubt my word." He flipped out a sack of tobacco. "It's bedtime for you, sis. Turn in and sleep all day if you can. Jim will bunk down on the couch."

Mary demurred, but Cope was stubborn, and she gave in. When he and Jim were alone, Cope smoked in silence, frowning.

Jim said suddenly, quietly, "Haynes took Ben Beauchamp, didn't he?"

Surprise flooded Cope's face. "I was tryin' to think how to tell you. How'd you know?"

Jim shrugged. "He wouldn't suspect you. You were the only man out of the office, the only one that had the chance to break me out. Besides Ben Beauchamp, that is. Where is Ben?"

"In the bank vault," Cope said quietly. "It's the only jail we got till the other's fixed."

"What's Haynes goin' to do about Ben?"

"Hold him for trial. Aidin' a murderer to escape."

Jim said gently, "Oh, no, he isn't."

"He's doin' it, ain't he?"

"Now, yes. But not for long."

Cope stared at him. "You mean you're goin' to break Ben Beauchamp out of that vault?"

"I am."

Cope didn't speak for a long moment, and when he did it was with bitterness. "You mean you'll risk gettin' shot—risk, hell! You will get shot! You mean you'll do that when you know how much we count on you?"

"I pay back my debts," Jim murmured.

"Debt? What do you owe that yellowbellied kid except

a kick in the pants for talkin' so much?"

"He wouldn't be in there if it wasn't for me."

"You'll break him out?"

"I will."

Cope sighed and then smiled gently. "I hoped you'd say that. I don't like it, but I like you for doin' it, Wade."

Jim found he was liking Jack Cope. When you got behind the wall of his toughness, you discovered that his single devotion to Mary Buckner had made a strange man of Jack Cope. He was human and compassionate, but as patient as an Indian, hard as granite, and more stubborn than a hunting dog. When he talked of Mary, his eyes lighted up, and his jaw set grimly, and a man understood without his saying it that she was his life. He talked about her now.

"How you goin' to crack Excelsior up, Wade?" he asked.

Jim shook his head. "I don't know."

"I'll tell you one thing," Cope said grimly. "If it was only me—or you—concerned in this, I'd take a gun and go choose Max Bonsell. After that I'd choose Harvey Buckner. But while Mary's in it, we can't do it."

"It may come to that."

"Maybe," Cope said. "It'll break her heart, though. She thinks she hates Harvey Buckner. But it ain't in the girl to hate a man the killin' way."

Jim leaned back in his chair and let Cope talk about her. But he wasn't listening. Minutes later, when Cope looked over at him and saw his inattention, the talk ceased.

Jim said then, "If we bust this open now, Cope, and beat Bonsell and Buckner, we'll have those squatters to deal with still, won't we?"

Cope nodded cautiously.

"How many of 'em?"

"Fifteen or so."

"And they'll fight?"

"To the last damn ditch."

Jim brought his chair to the floor and leaned across the table toward Cope.

"Who'll win this fight between the squatters and Bonsell?"

"Bonsell, of course. He's got 'em half licked now."

"Then why not let him lick 'em the whole way, shove 'em off, sweep the range clean? Why not let him do it now instead of us doin' it later? Because downin' Bonsell and Buckner is only half our job if Mary wants the Ulibarri grant. The squatters are the other half."

Cope regarded Jim with shrewd eyes. "How?"

"By crowdin' Max Bonsell so hard that he'll have to strike hard to save his life."

"You mean we side in with the squatters?"

"It'll look like that. And when Bonsell strikes, he'll strike at them."

Cope was silent a long moment. "It's risky. And Mary will hate it."

"What if it is?" Jim retorted. "And Mary won't have to know."

Cope said carefully, "If she finds out you're behind that, Jim, she'll hate you. It ain't that she isn't used to murder. She saw her daddy killed. But that's why she hates it. And what you're proposin' is murder and more murder."

"Not murder," Jim prompted. "Justice. A man pays for what he does. That crew killed Buckner in cold blood."

"But it's murder to her."

"Not to me."

"Nor to me," Cope murmured. He rolled another cigarette and smoked it down and then said, "I've got to get down to the saloon." He rose and tucked his stout crutch under his arm, which was as huge as an ordinary man's thigh. And then his chill blue eyes settled on Jim.

"That's our hole card, Jim," he said. "Play it."

Jim only nodded, and Cope stepped to the door, then paused. He turned to regard Jim. "It strikes me," he said, "that you see in Mary Buckner what I've seen in her, Jim." He held Jim's gaze. "If anything ever happens to me, I think you'll take up where I left off. Am I right?"

"I think you are," Jim replied. And that, both of them knew, was the bond that sealed them forever.

Chapter Seven: TWO CATS BY THEIR TAILS

AT MIDDAY, Cope let himself in with his key and wakened Jim.

"Bonsell is in town," Cope announced.

"He's got the nerve, all right."

"Ain't he?" Cope murmured, and swore softly. "He went straight to Haynes and offered to give himself up. But he asked one privilege before they locked him up."

"What was that?"

"To hunt you," Cope said, grinning wryly. "He said that he never suspected you was a killer. He said it made him sick to think of what you'd done. He said that although he'd been in town at my place the night the killin' took place, and although he'd never given the orders, didn't know anything about it, he was willin' to take his punishment. But he wanted to find you and kill you first."

"What did Haynes say?"

"What I told him to say," Cope said mildly. "I was there when Bonsell talked to him. I turned to Haynes and said, 'That's a white man's act, Link. I never liked Bonsell much, but I got to give him credit, he's shootin' square as a die with you.' When Link heard me say that, he said the same thing." He grinned. "So Bonsell walked out, free as air."

"What about his crew?"

"Paid them off and drove them off the Excelsior with a

rifle, he said."

"As far as the hills?" Jim murmured.

"Not that far, I reckon," Cope said. "As far as the second story of the house." He turned to go and then paused. "I dropped a letter to Harvey Buckner today."

"Saying what?" Jim asked, rising on an elbow.

"I didn't say much. Just told him if he aimed to keep the Excelsior, he better get up here. Max Bonsell was changin' boundaries on him just as fast as he could dig up the corners. I told him by the time he got up here, he'd find a ten-mile ribbon surveyed off two sides of the grant and home-steaded under Bonsell's name." He waved casually and hobbled to the door. "I've never tied two cats together by their tails, but I reckon I'll have a good idea of how they act when Bonsell and Buckner meet."

Jim was grinning a little as he dropped off to sleep.

At dark, he rose and quietly prepared himself a meal. Mary was still asleep, exhausted by the hard stage journey. When Cope came in, Jim asked for a gun, and when he got it he rammed it in his belt, saying, "Now tell me about the bank."

Cope said it was in the middle of the block on the same side of the plaza as the sheriff's office. It was adobe, but its vault was stone. The two front windows were heavily barred, as were both the rear and front doors—and the skylights. It was as escape-proof as a jail, more so on account of the vault.

"You mean they've closed the vault door on Ben?" Jim asked. "How does he get air?"

"Not the steel door, but the barred door. There's two of 'em."

"And how many men are in the place guardin' him?"

"Three."

"Can anybody get in?"

"Nobody but the sheriff and us deputies. The door and

windows are locked and hung with burlap." Cope grinned. "They figure he freed you last night so you'll try to pay him back. Haynes aims to make an example of the kid. It's a sort of advertisement that the law means business here in San Jon." He watched Jim's face, waiting for him to speak. When Jim didn't, Cope said, "How you goin' to do it?"

Jim smiled absently and put on his coat. "I'll tell you later," he said.

"What about horses?" Cope said.

"I don't know," Jim murmured. He grinned at Cope and stepped out into the night. The chill air smelled good, and he breathed deeply several times before he descended the stairs. Once in the alley, he tramped down it, whistling softly under his breath. A rider on horseback turned into the alley, coming toward him, and Jim passed saying, "Howdy," and getting a response in kind.

His first destination was the livery stable. This he achieved by keeping to the alleys and the darkness and crossing the streets without a second's hesitation. Few enough people had seen his face, and even they would not recognize him if they met him in the dark. Once in the alley behind the livery stable, he approached the feed corral cautiously. It had a few horses in it, one of which was Sleepy. He had heard Haynes give the man orders last night to take him there. The corral lot was dark, and there was only a dim glow in the stable's centerway. From the back end of it, he could look clean through it to the old man seated on his tilted chair, the lantern overhead. The old man was reading a newspaper.

Jim dropped deeper into the corral. The horses came up to him regarding him curiously, and then Sleepy, with a whinny of recognition advanced toward him. Jim looked back. The old man was still reading.

His next action was a strange one. Instead of petting

Sleepy, he ignored him and advanced toward another horse. The horse slowly backed off, and Jim crowded him into a corner. Sleepy watched this with something like amazement, and then when he understood that Jim was after another horse, his resentment conquered. He neighed shrilly and charged past Jim at the other horse. Jim vaulted for the poles just in time. Sleepy reared and slashed savagely with his teeth at the other horse, and the animal, cornered, fought back.

The thunder of their hoofs and their shrill cries rang clearly into the night. Sleepy had switched ends and was kicking at the other horse with loud and angry squeals. Jim watched the centerway. When he saw the light getting brighter, he knew he had succeeded. He streaked in between the stable and the corner building, making for the front walk. When he got there, it was dark, for the old man had taken the lantern back with him on the run to the fight. Jim strolled through the archway to the row of nails where the bridles hung, helped himself to one, and went back the way he came.

The old man had set the lantern on the dirt of the corral lot and was cursing Sleepy and the other horse with blistering invective. But you could tell it was a good-humored swearing, for the old man was smiling. Sleepy and the black had quit fighting, and Sleepy stood there looking foolish, his short ears laid back a little as if he were ashamed. He came over to the old man and had his neck scratched, and after that the old man picked up his lantern and went back to his chair.

The rest was easy. When everything was quiet, Jim went to the gate and whistled quietly. Sleepy, with not a second's hesitation, trotted over to him. Jim made up his slight to Sleepy in a few words and an ear scratching, then opened the gate. Sleepy followed him down the alley.

Jim adjusted the bridle and played Sleepy's stalling

game for a minute, then he mounted bareback, and they headed for the alley that was behind the bank.

Once there, Jim ground-haltered Sleepy and, from the vantage point of a woodshed, considered the proposition before him. The front and back doors of the bank were impregnable, locked tight and barred. That meant that even the windows were closed. But what about the skylights?

He sought the tallest woodshed, climbed it, mounted to the roof of a store, and crossed over on the other roofs to the bank.

There, on the angled roof of the bank, he could see a skylight. The one on the south slope was closed. He mounted the ridge and came down on the north side, and suppressed a grin of pleasure at what he saw. This skylight was open. Cautiously he peeped over the edge.

The window, on a chain, swung down far enough for him to see, directly below him, a table on which rested a kerosene lamp. A guard was reading a paper by its light, and off at the other end of the table the other two guards were playing double solitaire. The close heat welling out through the skylight was almost stifling.

Jim considered the setup for some time, then rose and went back to Sleepy. Fifty yards down the alley was the jail, and out of curiosity, Jim strolled toward it, a plan slowly taking shape in his mind.

The masons had been at work putting in a new back wall to the cell block. A great gaping hole still showed in its middle. Buckets of water, a mortarboard, a pile of stone, and some sacks of mortar were stacked neatly against the wall.

Jim stood there regarding Cope's handiwork, and a sudden grin broke his face. Stealthily, then, he crawled into the cell through the hole. Its door was open, so that he tiptoed through it and put his ear to the office door. He could see a pencil of light under the door, but no sound issued from the office. He stayed that way five minutes, listening, then gently twisted the knob of the door.

Poking his head inside, he saw that the office was empty. He entered, crossed to the lamp, which was turned down dim, and blew it out. Then he took off the lamp shade and, handkerchief for padding, removed the chimney. This he took with him as he went out the way he came.

At one of the buckets of water, he stopped and got a mouthful of muddy water, which he did not swallow. Down the alley by Sleepy, he carefully set the chimney on a woodbox, then, holding the water in his mouth, climbed to the roof again.

At the open skylight, he knelt again and considered the scene below him. Nothing had changed; one man was reading, and two were playing cards by the light of the single lamp.

Then he carefully leaned out over the skylight until he could see down the lamp chimney into the clean orange flame. He opened his mouth then, just a little, and let about a teaspoonful of water drop.

The effect was electric. The tiny bit of water plummeted down and hit the lamp chimney. When it touched, there was a brittle cracking and a jangle of glass as the heavy shade settled down on the lamp base, extinguishing the flame.

Jim ducked back, hearing a chair crash backward.

"Holy Mike!" one of the guards said. "That scared me. What happened?"

"The damn chimbley broke," the second said.

"We got another?"

"Hunh-unh."

"I better shag it over to the Emporium and get one."

"Nothin' doin'," the third guard said. "You stay here.

Flag down somebody on the street and tell them to tell Kling to send one over."

"Bueno."

Jim moved softly up to the false front of the building. He heard the door open, and then waited about a half minute until the tramp of a passer-by's boots pounded on the boardwalk.

Then he heard a man say distinctly, "Pardner, do me a favor, hunh? Our lamp chimbley broke. Tell Kling to send one over, will you?"

"Sure enough. Big size?"

"Biggest he's got."

Jim went back to the skylight. They had lighted the chimneyless lamp below, but it was just a guttering flame, no bigger than a candle flame.

He left the roof and retrieved his lamp chimney, then cut in between the bank and its neighboring building. After he judged enough time had passed, he put his hat under his coat and walked the ten steps to the bank door, where he rapped sharply on the glass. It was dark here, so that a man could not recognize his face.

The door opened a crack, and Jim said, "Here's the chimney you sent for."

"Good." A hand reached out to accept it. Jim dropped the chimney, grabbed the man's wrist, kneed the door open, and slipped in behind him, all in one motion. The second motion was to ram a gun in the man's back. The third was to close the door, shutting out the public.

"Quiet!" Jim whispered savagely. "Walk ahead."

Only one of the guards seemed attracted by the scuffling. He was closest to the lamp, on the other side of it, so that he could not see clearly.

"What's the trouble, Dave?" he asked, stepping out to see better.

Jim prodded the man in the back.

"Nothin'," Dave quavered. "I dropped the chimbley.

And by that time, Jim was among them. He did no speak. He merely stepped aside, Dave's gun and his ow in his two hands, and then held the guns leveled at th others.

He watched the surprise wash over the faces of the othe two. Slowly, the man who had been sitting came erect. H started to speak and found he had nothing to say, so swa lowed instead.

"One yeep out of the three of you," Jim murmured "and it'll make sixteen murders for me instead of thi teen."

He let that sink in. One of the guards stammered, "Yo —you're Jim Wade."

Jim nodded. "Put your irons on the table, boys. Dav you take 'em."

Dave did as he was bid. When the three of them wer disarmed, Jim called, "Ben!"

There was a sleepy mumble, and then, as if you coul see recognition take hold in Ben's mind, booted fee crashed to the floor, and Ben Beauchamp, a grin a yar long on his face, rushed to the bars.

"Jim!"

"Hi, kid," Jim said. To Dave he said, "Rustle up th key, Dave. Be quick about it."

Dave did. The key was on a nail in the wall, and Ji instructed Dave to open the door. When Ben stepped ou Jim said, "Now you three step in."

When one of them hotly demurred, Jim cocked his gu nothing more. The three of them went in, and Jim swun the barred door shut and locked it.

"Now the key to the back door," Jim demanded.

It was given him. "I'm goin' to shut this steel door s your yappin' won't be heard," he told them. "I'll giv warnin', though, and they'll be after you in ten minutes.

With that, he slammed the vault door and spun the dial. Immediately, the trio inside began to yell, but it was only the faintest of murmurs on this side of the door.

Jim looked over at Ben and grinned.

"I knew you'd be after me," Ben said, smiling broadly. "I dunno how I knew it, but I did."

Jim's face sobered. "Kid, this may mean the dark trails for you. They'll have reward dodgers out for you, like they'll have for me."

"Let 'em!" Ben said hotly. "They'll never catch me!"

"Where you goin'?" Jim asked.

"Wherever you go."

"But I'm stayin'."

"Then so am I."

Jim considered for a half minute. If he could watch over this kid, guide him, then the chances were in the end the kid would be free. But if the kid high-tailed it, dodging the law, it might be the making of a tough young outlaw. Either choice was bad, but when Jim thought of Lily, he knew he had to help the kid. Besides, he wanted to. He smiled and said, "Know a hide-out close?"

"Sure." The kid told him, and Jim approved.

Afterward, they slipped out the back door. Sleepy wasn't very enthusiastic about the kid, but when Jim spoke to him and hoisted Ben up on his bare back, Sleepy was docile.

Jim saw Ben ride off down the alley, turn past the jail at a walk, and slowly ride out of town.

Afterward, Jim hunted around for a brick. He found it, went back into the bank, blew out the light, and threw the brick through the front window. It collapsed in a jangle of glass. That was all the advertisement the three guards needed.

He slipped out the back way and took to the alleys again. He had negotiated two of them when he heard the alarm rouse the town. There were shouts, and dimly he heard men running.

Swinging into the alley, he was whistling softly. Its darkness and desertion assured him that the way to Cope's was clear.

He was thinking about Mary now, glad he was about to see her, when out of the night a voice spoke.

"Don't put a gun on me, Jim."

Jim's reaction was automatic. He whirled into the shelter of a shed, streaking up his gun, peering into that thick darkness. He could not see ten feet, and he remained deathly silent.

"Jim. Jim Wade!" the voice said again. It came from beside another shed.

"Light a match," Jim ordered.

There was a second's fumbling, and then a match flared. By its light, Jim saw the thin, bearded features of Scoville, one of the Excelsior gun hands. He cursed under his breath. "What do you want?" he asked coldly.

"To talk to you."

"Throw away your guns. Light another match and do it."

When this was accomplished, Jim walked over to him. He distrusted and hated the Excelsior crew. They were not well enough known to him to stand out as individuals. In the mass, they were killers. But on the other hand, Scoville had been with him that night at the Star 88. He had obeyed orders and had not fought Jim. He deserved a hearing.

"What is it?" Jim said coldly, seeing his small, slim shape in the dark.

Scoville answered quietly. "It's hard to say it, Wade. For a Mexican dollar you'd cut down on me."

"I would."

"Don't do it yet. I know where your hide-out is. I've

waited for you. I think I deserve a hearin'." The man's speech was mild, diffident, anything but the rough and surly speech of the average Excelsior hand.

"How did you find out where I was?" Jim asked.

"When I drifted into this country Cope fed me and found me a place to sleep until I got work. He's the only white man in the town. I figured as soon as you were broken out of jail, it was Cope that done it. So I watched his place and saw you come out tonight."

"What do you want?"

"To join you," Scoville said simply.

"Join me in what?"

"Whatever you aim to do." He cleared his throat. "I'm not a killer, Wade. I'm on the dodge for a mistake I made when I was a kid. Bonsell's kind of jobs are the only kind left for me. But I don't want 'em. I didn't know any more about that frame-up of Bonsell's than you did. It was only the crew Bonsell himself brought into the country that knew about it. The rest of us didn't."

"What have you got against Bonsell?" Jim inquired coldly.

"Just that frame-up," Scoville answered quietly, bitterly. "Does a man need any more?"

There was a long silence, during which Jim weighed the risk of this. Finally he said, "What do you figure I'm aimin' to do, Scoville?"

"Get even with Bonsell."

"You willin' to risk your neck to do it?"

"Day or night," Scoville answered simply. He waited a moment and said, "If it's too big a risk, Wade, I'll light a shuck. Nobody but me knows where your hide-out is, and they won't. I'll slip out of this country tonight if you can't use me. But if you can, I'd like to stay."

Jim almost smiled. He tried to remember what Scoville looked like, the face of the man, which would give him a clue to the man's character. But he was just another Excelsior hand in Jim's memory. Yet there was something about the man's voice, unafraid, sincere. It was the voice of a man who has worked with horses, gentle and patient and stubborn. And God knows he needed men, all he could get.

The nose of Jim's gun sank.

"I think I do need you," he said quietly. "Come along."

Chapter Eight: WHEN KILLERS FIGHT

THE BIB K WAS THE SMALLEST of the four remaining ranches on the Ulibarri grant. It was on the southern edge, as if Mako Donaldson, its owner, had not had the boldness to really trespass. The reason its two-room shack had been chosen for the meeting of the surviving squatters was a purely utilitarian one. It stood in the middle of a sagebrush flat whose growth was so thick that it advertised the coming of even a jack rabbit.

Will-John Cruver had called the meeting, and old Mako Donaldson and his boy had nothing to say about it. There were six others besides these three, four old men and two young. The windows were hung with tow-sack, and the door was closed. Two other young men stood guard out in the night.

When Mitch Boyd, alone, rode up to the shack, answered the challenge with a curse, left his pony tied to the poles of the corral, and entered the house, Will-John Cruver put his knife away and threw the piece of wood he was whittling into the fire. There were ten men present, twelve counting the sentries, thirteen altogether counting Custer, who was watching the Excelsior.

The cuts about Cruver's eyes had healed well, but there was still a tinge of green about them that gave him a purely baleful look. The mud that he had picked up in the fight with Jim Wade was not wholly combed out of his whiskers, and clotted the thick tangle of them. His hair was uncombed; but despite his slovenly appearance, his filthy clothes, he gave an impression of untold power. Sometimes gentle old Mako Donaldson suspected that Will-John was a throwback to primordial mankind. He was rawhide-tough, snarly as a beast, cunning as a hunting fox, and neither defeat nor victory seemed to change him. A good man to lead others.

Will-John Cruver thought so, too. When squat Mitch Boyd removed the water bucket from the bench and sat down on it as the only seat left, Cruver rose and spit in the fire.

"You're a fine damn collection of brush rabbits," he observed with hefty sarcasm, regarding each face as he spoke. "I can't see how you worked up the guts to leave your holes and come here tonight."

"You know damn well why we did," Mitch Boyd said.

Cruver grinned, and his beard did not part enough to show his teeth. "I do. All I got to do is rattle that old skeleton and you all step into line."

"What do you want of us?" Mako Donaldson asked, his gentle eyes resigned.

"To fight," Cruver replied bluntly.

"With what?" Boyd asked dryly.

"With a little more guts than you're showin' now," Cruver retorted. He walked over to the deal table and sat on it. It sagged under his muscled weight.

He said bluntly, "How many of us are there here tonight that killed Jim Buckner?"

It was intentionally brutal, for Cruver could not be otherwise. He enjoyed the winces of the older men, Donaldson, Boyd, Slocum, Harmony, and Reed. The younger ones were impassive; this was too old a secret to impress them, but it was one that cemented them together, old and young.

Mako Donaldson said bitterly, "Cruver, you're goin' to wave that flag once too often. You'll get a slug in the back."

"Not from you yellowbellies," Cruver said.

Mitch Boyd said, "Get to the point, Cruver. I ain't got a man at my place. Bonsell could burn it down and I wouldn't know it for a day."

"There you got it," Cruver said. "You pack of Nellies sit home at a window with your cattle bawling out in the corrals for feed. You got a shotgun beside you, a rifle on your knees, a week's grub on the table, and, if you're lucky, a few sticks of dynamite on the floor. You're too damn scared to sleep, even."

"I built my place," Boyd snarled, his broad Irish face flushing. "I'm damned if I'll let that bunch burn me out without a fight."

"What fight?" Cruver retorted. "You haven't fought yet. You just hope you won't have to."

Mako Donaldson put in dryly, "Just because they've wiped you out, Cruver, let the rest of us do it our way. If we don't guard our places, they'll burn 'em."

"And what if they do? There's more logs in the mountains, ain't there? There's more cattle to steal!" He swore tauntingly at them. "Bonsell's got maybe fifteen men. There's thirteen of us left. That's fairly even, ain't it?"

When they didn't answer, he went on, his voice hard and sneering. "What you jugheads don't savvy is that if we're to stay here, we got to carry the fight to Bonsell. What does it matter if he cleans our range and burns us out, as long as we down him? Because if we don't down him we're leavin' this country—if we got enough life in us to walk. He aims to kill so many of us that the rest of us will high-tail it. He's come near to doin' it now."

"But I spent ten years gettin' that place of mine and my herds!" Boyd snarled.

"All right. You might's well face the fact you've got to do it again," Cruver retorted. "Here or somewhere else. Would you rather start farther south in a country you don't know, or would you rather start here in a country you do know?"

"Here," Mako Donaldson said.

"Then fight!" Cruver said. "Just fight! This ain't goin' to be settled in the courts. Harvey Buckner is smart enough to know that he'd better stay out of a lawsuit or we might tell the court who he is. And we can't tell who he is without tellin' that we murdered Jim Buckner. So it'll be settled with guns. We hold the place now. The only way we can keep on holdin' it is to band up and wipe out Bonsell or anybody else Buckner sends in here. But we can't do it by takin' pot shots from our own windows at any jasper that rides onto the place."

Mako Donaldson listened in silence, his lined face bitter. After Cruver finished, none spoke. Mako said suddenly, "I wish to God we'd tried peaceful means with Jim Buckner instead of the way we did! I've regretted it all my life."

"Just part of your life," Cruver sneered. "You still got some more regrettin' to do."

Mako looked up at him, his glance unafraid. "You're a brute, Cruver. You haven't a heart or a mind or a conscience."

"Just the kill-or-be-killed instinct," Cruver agreed blandly. "Only this time my instinct happens to need you, Mako—and all the rest of you."

"And if we don't?"

Cruver smiled more broadly now, showing strong yellow teeth. "It ain't far to a U.S. marshal. And after I've told him who killed Jim Buckner, it ain't far to a new country. And I ain't afraid to start again, either, like the lot of you."

Mako said quietly, "I don't think we ought to let you leave this house, Will-John."

Cruver really laughed then. "Let me!" he echoed. "Hell! You can't stop me. If you put a slug through my head, I'd stand here long enough to nail five of you. And you're too damned afraid of your yellow hides to take the chance."

Mako regarded him with quiet bitterness, and then dropped his glance. "That's true—only too true, and you know it."

Cruver nodded cheerfully. It didn't matter a whit to him whether these men hated or liked him, as long as they did his bidding. And he had been patient with them up till now. But that would stop.

"I think I will go," he drawled, rising, "and when I go out that door you better start thinkin' how you can gang up on a U.S. marshal." He looked around. As he turned, a gun appeared in his hand. He cocked it loudly and said, "Anybody aim to stop me?'

None answered. He strode toward the door. One of the young men, Mako Donaldson's son, made a tentative grab for his gun, but Cruver only swiveled his weapon toward him and grinned.

"Come back here, Will-John," Mako said. "You've got us licked and you know it."

"Have I, Boyd?" Cruver asked.

Boyd nodded. "I never thought I'd see the day when I'd fight for you, Cruver, but I guess it's come," Boyd said quietly.

"I guess it has," Cruver agreed. "But not only—"

He ceased talking, cocking his head to listen. "Someone just rode in," he announced.

They were silent, a little tense, listening to the approaching footsteps of a man walking rapidly. The door opened to admit a young man in dusty Levi's.

"Well, what's happened, Custer?" Cruver asked.

"Plenty," Custer said. "There was a scrap went on over there."

Custer was the lookout posted by loose agreement of the squatters to report any activity at the Excelsior. It seemed that there had been a fight at the Excelsior. After the massacre of the squatters, it was common knowledge among them that Bonsell had cached five men in the second story of the Ulibarri house and had sent the rest into the hills, to make good his word to the sheriff. That these men were up there only temporarily, everyone knew. The five were there to guard Bonsell until, under the pretense of hiring an entire new crew, he could recruit more renegades. But something had happened. It was dark when it began. Bonsell was in the cookshack talking to the cook. Custer had seen that through his glasses.

Then all of a sudden a rifleman hidden down by the barn had begun to pour lead into the cookshack. He broke the lamp on the second shot. Another rifleman over by the stacks joined in. The five men up in the house tried to go to Bonsell's help, but a third rifleman stopped that. He poured lead into the door of the house so fast a rabbit couldn't have got out. Furthermore, he kept it up all the time the other two were harrying Bonsell.

"It looked to me," Custer continued, "as if some of those Excelsior boys out in the hills had it in for Bonsell. They waited until he was by himself, away from his guards, and then jumped him."

"Then what happened?" Cruver asked impatiently.

"Why, there was only one gun in the cookshack. While Bonsell was trying to reach the man in the stacks with it, the other man down by the barn snuck up and fired the shack."

What happened after that was a pretty close thing for Bonsell, Custer said. He stayed in the cookshack until it was nearly burned up. The Chinese cook decided he'd rather die by a slug than have the building fall in on top of him. He made a run for the house.

"And they never even shot at him," Custer said. "It was pretty plain they was savin' their bullets for Bonsell. They waited until it looked like Bonsell was goin' to be buried under burning timbers. And then he made a run for it."

"Did he make it?"

"He did," Custer said. "But I bet he thinks he's dead right now. His shirt was on fire, and he slapped at it as he ran. They shot his hat off. They shot the gun out of his hand. I'd swear they took both heels off his boots. He fell down once, and the slugs threw dirt in his eyes. He dodged like an Indian, but they kept kickin' up dirt in front of him. He made the door in one long dive and got splinters shot into his face from the doorframe. He stood in there and cussed so hard at them that all the grass died. After that, the three of them pulled out."

Cruver said slowly, "They did, eh? They could have killed him but they just wanted to scare him. That means they want more wages, and if I know Bonsell, he'll take his time givin' it to them." He looked around at these men. "Well, if you're goin' to fight, now's the time to do it, while they're fightin' among themselves."

"And that makes sense," Mako Donaldson said.

"Then hit the saddle," Cruver announced briefly.

Chapter Nine: RIVER OF DEATH

JIM, BEN BEAUCHAMP, AND PHIL SCOVILLE met at the appointed place above the Excelsior. Jim was the last to come, and he was grinning when he crept behind the screen of cedars.

Scoville said, "I've heard considerable cussin' in my time, but Bonsell's made my hair a little curly."

"He didn't like it much, did he?" Jim asked.

"Do you think we hit him?" Ben asked.

Jim shook his head. "He could run all right. A hit man doesn't run, not even if he's scared."

They smoked while discussing the probabilities as to what Bonsell would do. Scoville believed he would call the crew together and mop up on the squatters, providing he believed that the ambush was at Cruver's direction. As for his suspecting Jim, it was improbable, simply because there were three attackers. Even if word of Jim's breaking out Ben last night had reached Bonsell—an unlikely thing, for Bonsell had not been in town this day—that would account for only two of the three attackers. And Scoville was certain that Bonsell did not know of his own desertion. The men in the hills came and went as they pleased, their safety being their own lookout. No, Bonsell would believe the attack was made by three squatters and he would strike immediately.

Jim listened to Scoville's opinion and disagreed with it, simply because he thought Bonsell was a more cautious man. He'd wait for daylight to strike, Jim thought.

Finished with their smokes, they separated, each to watch the house from a different angle, for it was imperative that no move of Bonsell's be missed.

Alone, picking his way through the cedars, alert for any sound, Jim took stock of his fortunes so far. This was the first move in his plan. Scoville's advent was plain luck. Jim had taken him to Cope's and ordered him to shave his beard. Here was a man who, unrecognizable with different clothes and smooth-shaven features, could circulate without drawing suspicion. Moreover, here was the man Harvey Buckner would seek out. Besides that, Jim found himself liking the man. His sincerity Jim never questioned. When he was cleaned up, he had the gentle features of a man harried by circumstance, quiet to moroseness, but possessed of a dry wit and quick, aggressive mind. Tonight, with a bran ' of sharpshooting that amazed Jim, he had proven invaluable. But with only Scoville and a green kid, he had to buck Bonsell's crew and Cruver's. Could he do it? And the image of Mary rose in his mind to strengthen him and confound him. He had to do it!

He slipped into a piñon thicket on the ridge to the north of the house. By daylight he would know if his ruse to goad Bonsell into open war had worked or whether he must cast about for some other plan.

The lamps were lighted in the second story of the big house, behind pulled shades. The cookshack was entirely burned, an unsightly pile of dull-glowing ashes and twisted metal where it had once stood. Evidently, a conference was in session, for only a lone guard squatted by the big house's doorway.

Presently a man came down from upstairs and went down to the corral. He saddled and rode off west, toward the hills. That would be a messenger to the rest of the crew, and at the sight of him Jim's hopes kindled.

After that, there was nothing to do but wait. Jim squatted down against a piñon, rifle across his knees, and dozed and started and dozed again.

It was in waking from one of these dozes that he heard the sound of someone walking behind him. It was a man, for he could hear the uncertain steps he was taking on the rocky ground.

Jim sat utterly still, his nerves taut. This couldn't be Ben or Scoville, or they would have whistled. The man came on, and in that thick darkness passed no less than five feet from Jim. He was making no great effort to be quiet, nor was he crashing brush. When he sky-lined himself, Jim could see he was carrying a rifle slacked in his arms.

When he was past, Jim came to attention. He saw the man down the slope now, bellied down behind a boulder facing the house. The cigarette of the guard at the door glowed and faded in the night.

Jim watched an interminable while. And then, down by the creek, an owl hooted. It was a good imitation, but it wasn't the real thing.

The man understood, however. He raised his gun, sighting it for a long time on the rock. He fired then, the shot crashing the night down. The cigarette the guard was smoking arched slowly to the ground, and Jim knew the shot had killed him.

Immediately, as if all hell had let loose, a dozen rifles exploded into the night. From their flashes, Jim saw they had formed a rough circle and surrounded the Excelsior. The lights in the house were immediately extinguished, and afterward the first flames of fire began to lick up at the big barn.

Bonsell, squatted against the wall of a second-story room in which five bedrolls were stretched on the floor, looked up at the sound of that first shot. He held a knife in his hand with which he was picking splinters out of his leg by the aid of the lantern on the floor. He looked up at the four men, who were seated on the blankets watching him.

Without a word, he reached over and extinguished the lamp and said, "By God, they're back."

Lunging to his feet, he rapped out orders. "Spread out over the top floor. Ed and me will take the east side. Morg, you and Dutch take the west. And Dutch, you'll have to fight out the south end window, too."

There was a hurried tramping of feet as the men lunged for their rifles stacked in the corner. Bonsell, rifle in hand, plunged out the door into the long hall and came out in the north room. Already the window had been broken on the east side. To Ed, following him, he said, "Get over to that west window and fire at the gun flashes!"

He stood just beside the window now, looking out. They had already fired the big barn, and the smaller out-buildings were catching. It wasn't at this he was looking. He was counting the gun flashes. When he had spotted all within range, he went over to Ed's window and counted those, too, then called through the hall to Dutch to count the ones he could see between the ridge and the well house.

When he got the tally, he stood there, his face dark with fury, shaded softly by the glare of the fire coming through the gaping window. Thirteen men! That was too many for five men to fight, he thought.

Without a word, he started shooting at the gun flashes. His aim was careless. All he wanted to do was expend shells. When he had shot fifty times, he called across the room to Ed.

"Got any shells, Ed?"

"No."

"Go get some."

"What about my place here?"

"I'll take your side. It's so light on this side they're afraid to show."

Ed tramped out of the room. Bonsell glanced once at the burning barn and the outbuildings. The flames had turned night into day, until he could see the whole sur-rounding countryside. Then he crossed swiftly to the west window. The ridge behind the house was lighted so bright-ly that he could see every branch of every tree. Only the shadow of the house, mounting part way up the hill, was black and secret. A man looking down at the house from the ridge could see nothing, since the glare would be in his eyes.

He dropped his rifle, stepped out onto the gallery, climbed the railing, then swung down, hanging by his finger tips to the gallery porch.

Presently, when he had stopped swinging, he dropped. He lit as lightly as a cat and rolled over in the grass against the wall. Nobody had so much as shot at him.

In a moment he heard Ed's voice calling softly from above, "Max! Max! Where are you?"

The fools! he thought. They'd stick in that house wondering where he'd gone until Cruver and his crew set fire to it. Then they'd all be trapped like rats. He'd had one taste of that tonight, and he didn't want more. If only those four fools would put up a good fight, giving him time for what he wanted to do!

He lay there listening to the fury of gunfire all around him. Ed had gone back to his shooting. The fire was slowly dying, letting night creep in again.

When the light had dimmed enough so that the ridge was just a black blur again, Bonsell moved. He crawled through the grass until he had achieved a tree. Then, dodging from one tree to the next, he made his way up the hill, aiming at a place between two riflemen.

Once above them, he took out his six-gun and made his way straight to one of the squatters. In the darkness, no one could recognize him.

He came up behind the squatter and said, "Where are the horses?"

"Over the second ridge west. What the hell do you—"

Bonsell shot. The man simply folded in on himself and dropped his head. After that, Bonsell made his way back to the horses, the concert of gunfire gradually diminishing in volume as he walked.

He found the horses in an arroyo. The fools hadn't bothered to leave a guard with them. He led one horse aside, then took out his knife and methodically cut the cinches of every saddle.

Finished, he mounted and rode west, toward the hills. Not once did he think of those four in the house. They would serve their purpose, he hoped, if they contrived to stave off the burning of the house till daylight, giving him time to act.

Less than half an hour later, he met the rest of the crew pounding up the trail headed for the Excelsior. They pulled up around him as he waited. He didn't know whether or not they'd seen the flames from the burning buildings; he didn't care.

"We're ridin' out now!" he said harshly.

"They raid the place again?" someone asked.

"Yes. They caught the five of us. Put a knife in Blackie and sneaked upstairs. They got the rest of the boys. I made a dive out onto the gallery and jumped." He spoke in a casual voice that lent itself well to his mock heroics. "I got to their horses," he continued, "and cut the cinches. They're there for a while."

"Then let's go get 'em!" a man said.

"You'll do what I tell you!" Bonsell said coldly. "They can fort up on a ridge, mend the cinches, then turn around and chase us when they're done. We won't get anywhere that way."

"What do you aim to do, Max?" MaCumber asked.

"Strike!" Bonsell said sharply. "Split up into four bunches, and ride to the spreads we missed the other time. There's no one there now. I want you to burn their places first. After that, gather their cattle. They've pushed their beef close to the buildings already. I want you to drive that beef west, converging at Mimbres canyon. That's central to every spread left. Haze the stuff hard. If any of it lags, shoot it! I want every walking head of beef you find pushed to the Mimbres rim by noon. Do you get it? Then ride!"

Bonsell waited long enough to divide the men, then, heading one group himself, he set out for Boyd's place. They rode like fury, and reached it just at daylight. It was deserted. Boyd had pushed all his herds into the big horse pasture, and they were packed in like matches in a box, bawling their lungs out to be turned loose. As soon as the barns were fired, Bonsell directed the pasture gate to be opened, and as the hungry longhorns boiled out, his men skillfully directed them up the valley toward Mimbres.

It was a savage drive. The cattle were hungry and wanted to graze, but they were not allowed to. The stubborn ones were shot, and at the smell of their blood, the others became restive and wild. Bonsell tried every way he knew to start a stampede, and finally, when he killed a calf and dragged it past the flank, he succeeded.

It worked perfectly. There was no place for the cattle to stampede except up the valley. With two men on swing, keeping them bunched, there was nothing to do but ride. Other small herds were picked up on the way, and when these threatened to stop the stampede, Bonsell shot them. By midmorning the cattle had run themselves out, but the Excelsior hands harried them frantic. There was no lagging. The whole valley floor for miles was strewn with their warm carcasses. A little after eleven they approached the Mimbres rim.

Eons ago, a strong spring had started to gouge this valley out. Today it was a canyon two hundred feet deep, quite wide, with a grassy floor. Its sides were sheer dark sandstone, eroded first by water and later by wind. On its far rim, Bonsell could see two big bunches of cattle that his men had already gathered in. Letting his own big herd rest, he dispatched a messenger to the men across on the opposite rim. By one o'clock the last and fourth herd, huge and unwieldy, was pushed up to join his. The cattle were so tired they almost dropped in their tracks, and bedded down thankfully a half mile from the rim.

Bonsell drew his men off out of sight and let the milling herd quiet. The men smoked in silence, ears cocked for any sounds of pursuit. But the guards, stationed at high points of land, signaled everything was quiet.

Presently, Bonsell rose and said, "String out in a line. Anything that doesn't move, kill it. The signal to begin is a shot from me."

They mounted and, still out of sight of the tired cattle, strung out in a long line. When they were ready, Bonsell raised his gun and fired.

With a long Comanche yell, guns booming, the crew poured down onto the resting cattle. Harried, tense, nervous from too much running, it took little to startle the herd. The cattle took one look at these men pouring toward them, then heaved to their feet and started off in the opposite direction—which was straight for the Mimbres rim.

By the time the lead steers were approaching the rim and, sensing the danger, were trying to veer off to the south, the whole herd had got under way. Nothing could turn it, for blind panic guided its ponderous pushing.

In one thundering, bawling mass of moving backs, a mighty brindle sea flooded over the rim, stepping off into space and slowly arcing out to drop. Those in the rear pushed so hard that the ones in front were helpless. It flowed on and on, slow and majestic, to the rim, then continued in an unbroken line to drop thunderously to the canyon floor below.

Max Bonsell stood aside and watched it, his only thought being what a pity it was to destroy so much money. His glance at the opposite rim showed him that the two herds opposite were meeting a similar fate. His own signal to start the stampede had been the signal for them, also.

The last dozen steers in the drag refused to go over and had to be shot. Once it was done, the Excelsior crew dismounted and looked down at their handiwork. It was an awesome sight, so terrible a piece of destruction that it defied discussion. Already, the scavenger buzzards were collecting, wheeling overhead in motionless, hungry circles, probably wondering if their eyes deceived them.

The crew joined at the canyon bottom a mile to the south. Max Bonsell allowed himself a meager smile of satisfaction when he thought of it.

"Back to your camp, boys," he announced. "This will make Cruver's bunch so salty we'll be busy—or it'll take the heart right out of 'em."

Chapter Ten: QUIET—AND DEADLY

MARY BUCKNER, FOR DECORUM'S SAKE, had registered at the Exchange House the night she arrived. After catching up with her sleep at Cope's quarters, she went back to her room. The hardest part of her duty from now on would be the waiting. But for the first time since Uncle Jack Cope, roused to an injustice that strangled him with rage, planned to some day win back the Ulibarri grant for her, she was at peace. Perhaps it was Uncle Jack's confidence that at last he had found the man for the job, or maybe it was just Jim Wade's quiet way that gave her confidence. Anyway, she had it and she was happy.

When she thought of Jim Wade's breaking Ben Beauchamp out of jail, she shuddered a little with fright. She was glad that nobody had told her he planned it, and now that it was over she felt a little faint when she thought of what might have happened. But in a few words, Uncle Jack had made her see why it was necessary.

Still, there was so little she could do. Nobody in this town knew her. Only a handful could remember her, and she could remember none of them, except Jack Cope. But when Jim Wade rode out of San Jon he had left certain instructions with her, instructions as elaborate as they were preposterous. She determined, however, that she would carry them out to the letter.

That was what brought her into Kling's emporium, on this afternoon, for thread and needles. Mr. Kling himself, who remembered her, waited on her. She shook hands with him, and, after some indecision on his part, he inquired after the health of her father. He understood, of course, that this might not be polite, since James Buckner had simply skipped the country in the middle of the night, leaving his daughter to be raised by a saloonkeeper and his wife. Mary answered his inquiry offhandedly.

"I'm sure I don't know, Mr. Kling," she said. "You know as much about him as I do."

It was a cool answer and it put Kling in his place. He resented her tone and recalled with considerable satisfaction what a little liar she used to be. All the old timers remembered that whopper she had told on the night James Buckner left San Jon—about him being murdered by some of the cattlemen near here. Some of the old fogies even believed it for a while, until James Buckner turned up in Santa Fe. Men who remembered him had seen him down there. He was a changed man, maybe a little crazy. Certainly he had a pretty daughter, though, even if she was a little uppish and inclined to stretch the truth.

But Mary's smile soon won him over. She was in trouble, she said.

"What trouble?" Kling inquired kindly.

"I want some dresses made, Mr. Kling. Do you know of a dressmaker in town?"

"Why, there's two of them. There's Mrs. Benson. My wife goes to her, I think. Then there's Lily Beauchamp. She's young and flighty, but she needs the money powerful bad."

"Does she do good work?" Mary wanted to know.

"I—I—not so good as Mrs. Benson," Kling said honestly. "But she does need money. Well, these things are pretty simple to make. Perhaps I ought to give her my trade," Mary said.

"That's right kind of you, Miss Buckner," Kling said, and proceeded to tell Mary where Lily Beauchamp lived.

All this was to advertise the fact that the meeting of Mary Buckner and Lily Beauchamp was purely by accident. Jim Wade and Cope both needed Lily in their scheme and had her promise through Ben that she would help. Scoville, who was posing as a saddle tramp wanting work, was to live there. It would afford him a place to live and her protection in Ben's absence. With Mary's introduction to Lily, this small band of conspirators would be as tight-knit as possible, and yet their associations must seem casual and accidental to the public.

Ten minutes after Mary left Kling's, she was knocking on Lily Beauchamp's door. Lily opened it, and for a moment these two women looked at each other, and with none of the animosity of their sex.

"I'm Mary Buckner."

"I know. Come in, please."

Once the door was closed, Lily smiled. "I've heard so much about you through Ben, who heard it through Jim."

"And I about you from Jim," Mary replied. "He hasn't forgotten your willingness to help him—and thought it might include me."

Lily's weary face lighted up at the mention of Jim's name, and in a flash Mary Buckner knew that this girl loved Jim Wade. And why shouldn't she, Mary thought, after what Jim had done for her brother Ben? All the same, Mary felt a pang of jealousy, for Lily Beauchamp was a pretty girl, and a nice one.

Once seated, Lily asked shyly if Mary would tell her the whole story. What she knew now had come from Ben, in two- and three-minute-snatches when he sneaked into the barn at night to see her. Mary told her story, and when she was finished, Lily nodded gravely.

"I think Cope was right in picking Jim. He—he can do it if anyone can, Miss Buckner."

"You love Jim Wade, Lily?" Mary asked simply.

Immediately, that cold mask of defiance settled on Lily's face, and her eyes were angry, but when she looked at Mary, she saw only another woman, a kind woman, who understood her secret already. She only nodded, pleating the cloth of her dress with nervous fingers, watching Mary.

"Are you ashamed of it, then?" Mary asked.

"No," Lily answered abruptly. "I never would be. Only —only I don't think he loves me."

A gladness stirred in Mary that she was immediately ashamed of. "He speaks kindly of you, Lily," she said.

"He does of his horse, too," Lily said, with tired irony. "It's—well, he just doesn't need a woman." She watched Mary's face, and could see only sympathy in it, and she was not afraid to go on. "He's different, Miss Buckner. He—"

"Mary, Lily."

"But he is, Mary. That night out in the street in the rain, I saw it, and I understood how different. Men look at him and they are in his power, whether they know it or not. Any man in that crowd of toughs that night could have pulled a gun on him and danced him out of town, with everyone laughing. Only they didn't. They were afraid to. He never raised his voice, didn't even make a threat, but they were afraid of him. That's what Jack Cope saw, what I saw, what Ben sees."

Mary nodded, intent upon the soft loveliness of Lily's face as she spoke of Jim. When Lily was finished, Mary said softly, "And you think I'm selfish in asking him to help me, Lily?"

"I didn't say that!" Lily said.

"But you think it, don't you? You think I am a lucky woman already, with a job and an education and enough

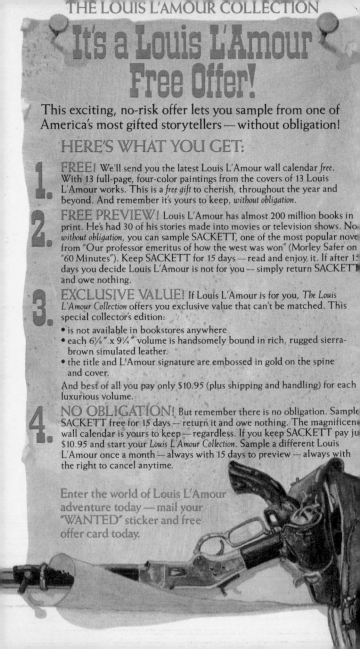

FREE — MAGNIFICENT WALL CALENDAR!
FREE — PREVIEW OF SACKETT
- No Obligation! • No Purchase Necessary!

Yes! I'm claiming my reward!

Send SACKETT for 15 days free! If I keep this volume, I will pay just $10.95 plus shipping and handling. Future Louis L'Amour Westerns will be sent to me about once a month, on a 15-day, Free-Examination basis. I understand that there is no minimum number of books to buy, and I may cancel my subscription at any time. The Free Louis L'Amour wall calendar is mine to keep even if I decide to return SACKETT.

NAME _____

ADDRESS _____

CITY _____

STATE _____ ZIP _____

MY NO RISK GUARANTEE:

There's no obligation to buy. The free calendar is mine to keep. I may preview SACKETT and any other Louis L'Amour book for 15 days. If I don't want it, I simply return the book and owe nothing. If I keep it, I pay only $10.95 (plus postage and handling).

70136

"WANTED!" STICKER GOES HERE

IL 1

Track down and capture exciting western adventure from one of America's foremost novelists!

- It's free! • No obligation! • Exclusive value!

good looks that a good man will marry me and take care of me. And instead of being satisfied, I want more. I want a huge land grant, property, power, and influence, to live like a great lady. And you think I've persuaded Jim Wade to risk his life to get it for me, don't you?"

Lily was agonized with embarrassment when Mary began, but when she was finished, Lily was calm, level-eyed, unafraid.

"Do you know what you've asked him to do?" she asked.

Mary nodded mutely, knowing what Lily would say. She had said it to herself a thousand times since that morning she had asked Jim Wade's help.

"He's a fugitive now," Lily went on. "There are ten thousand dollars in the bank waiting for the man who walks up behind him and shoots him. Or catches him asleep and shoots him. Half this town is still in the saddle, scouring the country for him. They hate him here, hate him because he is better than they are. He isn't safe a minute." She paused. "All that has happened to him because he wants to help you."

"But a lot of that happened before I asked him, Lily."

"No. If you hadn't asked him, he could have ridden out of here to safety. But now he stays, with one eighteen-year-old boy and a saddle tramp to help him."

Mary's glance wavered.

"I wasn't going to say this, but you guessed it," Lily said quietly, implacably. "Yes, I think all those things about you. And why shouldn't I? Aren't they true?"

"But can't you understand that getting this grant back is my life, everything to me—and to Jack Cope? It belongs to me! I'm part of it! My father died on it and is buried on it! It's been my dream, the only thing that's kept me going for years!"

"No," Lily said quietly. "The only thing I can understand is that it will mean Jim Wade's death."

"No!" Mary cried. "That's not so!"

"Max Bonsell has a dozen killers out there at the Excelsior. Sooner or later, he'll see that he and his men have to kill Jim Wade or be killed. Will-John Cruver has a dozen men, too. And sooner or later they will see they have to kill Jim Wade. That's twenty-five men against one—not counting your uncle and the sheriff and all these men in San Jon that Jim Wade has made a fool of!" She ceased talking, waiting for Mary to speak. "How great a man do you think he is?" she asked quietly. "It only takes one lucky bullet to kill him."

Mary, her lips pale, only shook her head and said nothing.

"If you only loved him," Lily said softly, wonderingly, "then I could understand. A woman in love thinks there's nothing her man can't do for her. But you haven't even that excuse. You want a piece of land. You haven't the money to pay for it. So you catch a man—a good man—in the heat of anger and ride to glory on his revenge."

"Lily, Lily," Mary murmured, her eyes wide in horror. "How you must hate me!"

The hardness drained out of Lily's face. "I don't," she said. "I don't know why it is, but I don't."

"Is there anything I can do now?" Mary asked. "You've —oh, it's true. I see it now! I was ashamed of it when I asked him, but somehow I didn't realize what I was asking." She looked up at Lily. "What can I do, Lily?"

"Has Jim promised you that he'll see it through for you?"

"Yes."

Lily said slowly, her voice resigned, "You can't do anything, then—except pray."

When Mary was gone, Lily got to work again. Now and then, out of pity, people brought her sewing to do, because Tom Beauchamp's drinking was a legend in the town.

Tom worked like a slave at his blacksmith shop during the day and drank all the night. Along toward morning he would stumble home, a violent-tempered man who could not understand his children, and who still grieved over the death of his wife these ten years past. Lily hated him with a passion, but it had been Tom Beauchamp's own idea that he fix up a room in the blacksmith shop for his own. He seldom came near the house, or contributed money to its support, and while it put a poverty on Lily and Ben that was breaking them, she was thankful she was spared her father's company.

She knew the small sewing jobs were charity, and she was clumsy at her work, but she would accept any crust thrown her because it was her only living. She knew she should have been glad at the news that Scoville was going to take a room here, glad of the money it would bring. But Mary's visit had unraveled again those memories of Jim Wade which she was so careful to knit up each day and lock away in that storeroom of hopeless longings. Not by any look or word had Mary Buckner betrayed that she loved Jim Wade. But how could a man look upon Mary Buckner and not love her? She was lovely and kind, the sort of woman a man could gladly die for. And sooner or later, Lily thought bitterly, Jim Wade would want to die for her. He had all but offered to now. Lily didn't blame Mary for what she'd done. After all, Mary Buckner did not know men like she did.

It was full dusk when a knock on the door startled her. It was Scoville whom she had talked to with Ben behind the shop night before last.

She invited him in and then lighted the lamp, afterward turning to observe him carefully. He had a friendly, sober face that was lighted by a shy smile. He was slight, almost frail-looking, dressed in tattered but clean Levi's and a gray flannel shirt. He carried his war bag in his left hand.

"I'll show you your room," Lily said, smiling a little.

She went into the passageway connecting the living-room with the kitchen. Two tiny rooms opened off the passageway, one her room, the other Ben's, now Scoville's.

Scoville looked at it and said, "It's been a long time since I saw a bed like that, Miss Beauchamp. I'll sleep on the floor till I get used to the idea."

Lily laughed. "It's held together by haywire, and the springs have been patched in a blacksmith shop. Ben always claimed that the mattress slept like Dad lost an anvil in it."

Phil Scoville laughed easily, and Lily joined in. He put his war bag on the floor, and Lily left him.

She went out into the tiny lean-to kitchen to make supper, thinking that Scoville, like Ben, would while away the time till supper by himself. But he was on her heels, standing in the doorway while she lighted the lamp. She saw him glance at the woodbox, which was empty, then he asked, "Where's your ax?"

"Next to the shop."

Scoville went outside. By full dark, he chopped enough wood to fill the box to overflowing. Then he sat down at the small table and watched her get supper. It had been a long time since Lily had had this kind of company, and she found herself talking with him about things she didn't know she remembered.

In one of the pauses, Scoville said, "Miss Beauchamp, this is kind of awkward to ask, but I aim to ask it, anyway."

"What's that?"

"Ben said your father slept in the shop. Don't my comin' make it sort of—bad for you?"

Lily smiled fleetingly. "I can't lose a reputation when I haven't one, can I?"

Scoville's eyes narrowed. "You've got one with the only folks that count around here."

"And who are they?"

"Jim, Cope, Mary Buckner, Ben, and me."

"Then why worry, if that's so?" Lily murmured.

"I reckon that's right, too," Scoville murmured. "Only, in stories and things like that, people meet you. How will they meet you? That's the question."

"Like they always have," Lily said gravely. "As if I were drunken Tom Beauchamp's trashy daughter."

"Then they better change their ways," Scoville murmured.

Lily turned away, something choking up in her throat. She finished getting supper, and during it they talked of Jim Wade. Scoville told Lily of the fight at the Excelsior, and of Bonsell's swift revenge. The herds of all those squatters remaining, except Will-John Cruver's, were so depleted that there seemed no reason for them to hang onto their claims on the Ulibarri grant. In some ways, Scoville said grudgingly, Max Bonsell was a genius. In this particular brand of hell-raising, especially so.

When Scoville had finished, Lily said, "Then Jim's idea is to fight them both, but in a way so that the evidence points only—"

"To Bonsell when it happens to Cruver, and Cruver when it happens to Bonsell."

"That's cruel, Phil," Lily said gravely after a pause.

"I know it," Scoville said. "It's cruel people you're doin' it to."

It was an evasive answer, but Lily saw that discussion of it made him uneasy, and she changed the subject.

Scoville helped her clean up after supper, then went into his room. He was riding out tonight.

There came a quiet knock on the front door, and Lily went through the hall to answer it.

Scoville heard the door open. There was a short silence, then Lily said coldly, "What do you want?"

"Hello, Lily," a thick and drunken voice greeted her. "Just wanted to see you."

"I don't want to see you," Lily said. "Go away."

There was a quick scuffling and then a deep laugh. "I reckon you do, after all."

Scoville quietly slipped down the passageway to the door. Will-John Cruver, drunk and filthy, was just inside the room. Lily had backed off against the table, her back to Scoville.

Scoville said flatly, mildly, "And I reckon she don't."

Cruver squinted over at him, no surprise in his face, only a little irritation. "Who's that? That damn Ben?"

Lily said faintly, "A man who rooms and boards here."

"Well, get back in your room and board, then, fella. I didn't come to call on you."

Scoville walked around the end of the table and stopped there, his legs spraddled a little. His face was white, tense. "You didn't come to call on anyone, mister. You got the wrong house on the wrong street in the wrong town. Try and find the right one."

Cruver looked over at Lily. "Who is he?"

"I told you," Lily said.

"Someone in ahead of me, huh?" Cruver drawled.

Scoville walked up to him and hit him in the face. Cruver's head rapped back against the wall with such force that a picture crashed down off its nail. He shook his head a little, while Scoville opened the door.

"Get out before I cloud up and rain all over you," Scoville drawled.

For one brief instant, amazement flooded into Cruver's face. Then his hand made a dip for his gun, and Lily cried out, "Watch out, Phil!"

But Scoville's two guns whipped up. With his right one, he struck down viciously at Cruver's wrist. It caught Cruver's gun half out of its holster, and there was a muffled,

ickening sound of grating bone. In the same second, he
aad swung his left gun in a tight, swiping arc and its
barrel connected sharply with Cruver's temple. Cruver
simply sat down, jarring the house, and his head sagged
on his chest.

Scoville looked up at Lily. "He isn't really a friend of
yours, is he?"

Lily was too frightened to answer. That this frail man,
so quiet and unassuming, should have been able to do
his, she could not understand. But there was Cruver on
he floor, and there was Phil Scoville, his eyes smoldering
out a thin smile on his face, regarding her.

Scoville said, "I think I better do this up right." He
aanded one of his guns, butt first to Lily. "Can you use one
of these?"

"Why—yes."

"Then if he ever sets foot in this place again, use it." He
miled more broadly now. "I'll take care of him. You go
back to your work."

Lily watched him haul Cruver out the door by the simple means of grabbing his dirty hair and dragging him. He
shut the door after him.

Lily waited until the sound had died, then she slipped
out the door. Scoville had rounded the rear corner of the
blacksmith shop and was headed for the plaza. When she
aad gained the vantage point of the hotel corner, she saw
Scoville still dragging Cruver across the road toward the
sheriff's office.

But in front of it he stopped. Suddenly she understood.
There was a big, cast-iron watering-trough in front of the
sheriff's office.

Scoville stooped down, picked up Cruver, and dumped
aim in the trough. At the sound of the splash, the door to
he lighted sheriff's office opened.

She heard Scoville drawl, "My landlady don't like muck

like this clutterin' up her house, Sheriff."

There was a pause while Link Haynes came down to regard Cruver, thrashing and coughing in the water.

"And who is your landlady?" Haynes asked mildly.

"Miss Lily Beauchamp," Scoville said. "When that slob gets real awake, you might tell him I'm always willin' to oblige my landlady."

Haynes, a wise man in more ways than one, said quietly, "I'll do that. I sure will."

And Scoville tramped off down the street. Lily returned to the house, her face rather thoughtful and glowing.

Chapter Eleven: BLOOD-SICK

JIM WADE ASCENDED COPE'S STAIRS with dragging steps. He came up softly, as was his custom, but on the platform he paused, his hand on the door. He was a long time opening it, and then he seemed reluctant to do so.

Cope and Mary were in the kitchen, but Cope's sharp ears caught the sound of the opening door. Mary was behind him, and she greeted Jim with a smile that should have warmed him. It did not, however.

"You're hungry, aren't you, Jim?" Mary asked.

Jim smiled crookedly. "I can't remember when I ate last, Mary."

Cope looked shrewdly at Jim and knew that something was wrong, but he did not speak of it. While Mary fixed supper, Jim smoked morosely in the tiny kitchen, and Cope, quick to step in the breach left by Jim's taciturn mood, gossiped in his gruff and rumbling voice.

But the food did not seem to raise Jim's spirits. His gray eyes were clouded, his face so haggard that Cope knew it was not entirely from saddle weariness.

Finished, Jim shoved his chair back from the table and packed his pipe.

Cope said with broad meaning, "Don't you reckon it's time you went, Mary, and let Jim get some sleep? He's wore out."

Before Mary could answer Jim looked up at Cope and said, "Let her stay, Cope. She might as well hear this now. Because it's finished."

Mary looked from Cope to Jim, and Cope avoided her eyes. "What's finished?"

It was Jim who answered her. "We had a fine plan, Mary. We couldn't tell you about it because"—he looked at Cope—"it was a little too rough."

"A plan? For what?"

Cope said gruffly, "How did you think Jim was movin' against Bonsell, Mary?"

"I—I didn't think he was," Mary said in a small voice. "From what I've heard, Bonsell's men and Cruver's are fighting each other. I thought we were waiting for Uncle Harvey's coming."

"They are fightin' each other," Jim said carefully, "because I set 'em at each other." He still looked at Cope. "But I'm finished with that. I can't do it, Cope."

Cope said nothing, and Jim presently told Mary what had happened so far, sparing himself no blame. His scaring of Bonsell at the Excelsior had been a little too expert. With Cruver's surprise raid it had infuriated Bonsell to the point where he was burning and plundering the squatters' range like a man gone mad. Withholding nothing, Jim told her in blunt words of the beef drive which, in one savage and lightning move, had practically destroyed the squatters.

"As close as I can figure it," Jim said tonelessly, "Bonsell left those four men to die in the house while he escaped. And that's what he did when he was free."

"Isn't that what you wanted?" Cope asked slowly.

Jim nodded. "But not any more, Cope." He stroked the

bowl of his pipe with his thumb, his eyes lowered, talking in a level, dead voice. "You see, I know the whole story now. I was there when those squatters—there were a dozen of 'em—rode up there to the rim of the Mimbres and saw what had happened. I saw them talk. I saw that sight kill them, Cope. There was half a lifetime's sweat and blood for them piled in rotting flesh on the bottom of that canyon." He raised his glance to Cope, and it was tortured, pleading for understanding.

Cope avoided his glance. "War is never pleasant, Jim. You know that."

"I thought I did," Jim murmured gravely. "But it takes a stronger stomach than mine."

This was something new to Mary. She heard his story with expressionless face, inwardly appalled at what Jim was telling. Intuitively, she understood that it had been a desperate move on Jim's and Cope's part, the only move whereby they could conquer against these odds. And now she was watching Jim Wade's conscience work, reaching blindly for a justice that was not in the cards. The fight at the Excelsior had not been of Jim Wade's making, but it might have been, and Jim Wade understood that. And being the man he was, he shrank from more of it, a just man turning from an infamy that he could not bear.

But Jim was talking now to Cope. "I even followed them up to that sorry camp they made in the hills, Jack. They built a big fire and huddled around it like kids, numb from what they had seen. If any of Bonsell's men had happened to ride past there then, he could have killed the lot of them before they could have made themselves move."

"They killed Mary's father," Cope said doggedly.

"I thought of that, watching them." He paused, and then burst out, "But they're so helpless, Cope! They don't know what they're fightin'! They don't even know how to go about it!"

He leaned across the table, talking earnestly, desperately now. "I sat there at first, watching them, thinking, 'All I've got to do now is drop word to Max Bonsell where to find them. Then it'll be over.' And when I thought that, I was sick."

"They killed Mary's father," Cope repeated stubbornly.

"Yes," Jim murmured. "Those poor blind fools and the sons they've raised. Fifteen years ago, drunk with their own desperation, they murdered a man. They killed Mary's father. And for fifteen years, it's haunted them. But they've married wives and raised children, Cope. They've built places, even if those places were on the land they murdered a man to get! They've sweated and ridden in rain and snow and gone hungry and watched their herds die in drouth! They've buried their wives on that land! They've saved and sacrificed to buy ten more cows next spring!" He paused, regarding Cope's implacable face. "Cope," he said softly, "you know those men. You know them by name. You've lived with them, sold them liquor to cheer them up in those black times that every cowman knows. Would you put a gun to the head of a one of them and pull the trigger if you had the chance?"

"Only Cruver," Cope murmured.

"And he's only one. There's others. There's one old man that has the face of a saint. He's suffered. To look at him, you know the murder of Jim Buckner has never been far from his mind these fifteen years."

"Aye. Mako Donaldson."

"Does he deserve a dirty bushwhacking at the hands of Bonsell?" Jim asked passionately. "He's paid his debt a thousand times over!"

"No," Cope answered. "He doesn't."

Jim leaned back and raised his glance to Mary. She wanted to help him, to cry out that he was right, but Jim Wade was blind to her tonight. He lighted his pipe in that stillness and began to talk again.

"Today I rode over to see where Bonsell was," he said softly. "I found his camp. It was deserted. I began to think then. I trailed a pair of his riders, Cope. From a break in the timber above Mule Springs, I saw enough to know what's happening. I saw two men forted up in the rocks, one sleepin', the other on watch. They were waitin' for someone. To make sure, I traveled over to the old stage road that leads to the west slope. I saw two more men. Waitin'." He smiled meagerly. "They've got this country bottled up, Cope. And when they see that this bunch of broken squatters are not goin' to run, they'll hunt 'em down. In two more nights, Cope, an Excelsior rider will spot that fire. And what will be the end?"

Cope's tough old face was sweating, his eyes sad and wise and touched with disillusion.

"But they've got to go, Jim," he said patiently. "Pity or no pity, they've got to go. Men build rules for a game and they name those rules law. And the man that breaks that law has got to pay."

"But not that way!" Jim said swiftly. "Not hunkered down over a can of coffee, lost as a damn sheep in a blizzard, when a slug takes him in the back! Not that way, Cope!"

"No, not that way. But what way?"

Jim only shook his head and smoked in silence, his face shaped by a sadness that made Mary's heart ache.

"When a man's young," Jim murmured, "he's got an answer for everything. A thing has got to be right or wrong, it can't be half-and-half." He looked over at Cope. "I'm not old, Cope, but I know this. Nothing is wholly right. Nothing is wholly wrong." He looked at his hands. "I've got to take those men out of the country," he said softly.

Cope's head jerked up. "*You* have got to!" he repeated.

"Why?"

"Because they can't get out by themselves."

"How do you know they want to go?"

"They've *got* to go," Jim said.

Cope smiled wryly. "Does it look like they want to go? Scoville pistol-whipped Cruver tonight for breakin' into Lily Beauchamp's house. He's down in my saloon, drinkin' up the guts to hunt Scoville down. Does that look like they wanted to leave? When they'll follow a man like Cruver?"

Jim's head jerked up. "Cruver's downstairs?"

Cope nodded. "And he'll be down there till he gets so drunk I throw him out."

Jim stared at the wall in front of him, something like hope flooding his face. Then he came to his feet, alert and smiling narrowly.

"Don't you," he drawled. "You keep him here, Cope. Can you do it?"

"Yes. Why?"

Jim reached for his hat, which he had put on the floor beside the table.

"Because that's all I need. With Cruver out of the way, I can swing it. I can take them out of here."

"They'll cut you to doll rags when they see you!" Cope growled. "They think you were in that first set of killin's, Jim." He stood up, steadying his massive body by grasping the back of the chair, too agitated to grope for his crutch.

"They'll listen," Jim said softly, "because they've got to listen."

"Jim," Mary said.

He looked over at her, almost as if she were a stranger. His face softened a little at sight of her.

"Don't go," she said. "Give it up! Jim, I didn't know what I was doing when I asked you to help me! I didn't know it would be this! I'll go away, Jim." She came close to him, and her eyes were wide with pleading. "Do you think my land, any piece of land, is worth all this blood? I'd rather be poor all my life than have the grant at this cost. You can't go, Jim! You can't!"

Jim shook his head and said gently, "It's too late, Mary. None of us—you nor Cope nor I foresaw it. But if I don't go tonight, it'll be worse."

He looked over at Cope for one brief instant, then wheeled and tramped through the room and left.

Mary stood immobile, watching him go, and then something died in her eyes. She stood there until Cope put his arm around her shoulder. It only needed that friendly touch for her tears to come. She turned and buried her face in his shoulder, sobbing until Cope thought her heart was broken.

"It's my fault," she said bitterly. "Oh, Uncle Jack, why didn't you tell me it would be like this?"

"I didn't know, child," Cope murmured.

"But they'll kill him! He'll go to them with kindness, and they'll kill him!"

"That they won't," Cope said softly. "He walks with a proud walk, girl." He stroked her soft hair, soothing her. "There's men and men, Mary. There's the kind that's born to die by the gun, and they're well dead. But there's a kind that's born to live by the gun, and out of all their violence there comes somethin' a man can build on. Jim's that kind. Men don't shoot at him, Mary. They listen to him."

Mary's sobs had ceased, and Cope knew she was listening to him. He wished he could wholly believe what he had told her, but that old hope was almost dead in him. But he could make it live for her.

"I—I hope you're right, Uncle Jack," Mary stammered.

"Of course I am," Cope said gruffly. "Now dry your eyes, girl. We've got to clean up this table."

Jim rode hard to reach the squatters' hide-out before sunup. False dawn was just laying its gray touch on the land when he ground-haltered his horse beyond the canyon mouth. There would be a guard posted halfway down this box canyon. This death trap these men had chosen as their fortress.

He moved slowly, picking up a landmark soon, a big boulder which the guard had chosen for his station. Jim had seen him last night. He circled the boulder, clinging to the soft dirt slope of the canyon side, and coming down behind it.

From there on he faced the rock and walked boldly toward it, not troubling to smother his footfalls. When he reached the rock, he saw the blurred shape of a man prone at the base of it.

He stood above the man, a high, flat figure in that chill morning air, and a wry smile played over his face. The man was asleep. Jim knelt by him and took the rifle from his side and then slipped his six-gun from its holster, afterward shaking him gently.

The guard roused with a start. "What is it?" he asked swiftly, peering up into Jim's face.

"Let's go back to camp," Jim suggested mildly. "I want to talk with your boys."

"Who are you?"

"Jim Wade."

The guard made a lunge for his rifle, and Jim gently placed the barrel of his gun in the man's chest.

"Not a move," he said, still mildly. "I only want to talk. Only I don't want you blowin' off your mouth before I get the chance. I'll have to hit you if you do."

The young puncher swore darkly and climbed to his feet. The east was gray now, so that a man could make out the shape of a tree.

"Let's hurry," Jim suggested.

Walking a step behind the puncher, Jim followed him up the canyon bed until, rounding a shoulder of rock, they were in the camp. It nestled at the very base of the box canyon's rear wall. A more perfect death trap to defend could not have been chosen.

In the coming dawn, Jim could see a man stooped over a small fire, nursing it with sticks.

He was Mitch Boyd, and, still bleary-eyed from sleep, he growled a good morning to the guard without looking at him.

Jim walked over and scattered the fire with a kick, his booted foot missing Boyd by inches only.

Boyd jumped backward, an oath on his lips, and then he saw Jim holding a gun on him, and his curse died.

"Nothin' like tellin' Bonsell where to find you, is there?" Jim drawled. "On this mornin' you could see camp smoke for ten miles."

Boyd's mouth dropped in amazement.

Jim gestured with his gun. "You two stand right here." The others were scattered in a loose circle about the fire in their blankets. Jim passed between them, lifting a gun where he saw it and feeling gently under blankets when he did not see one where it should be.

Finished, he stepped off to one side of the camp and said, "Better roll 'em out."

Boyd called, and the men tumbled out of their blankets. It was a full minute before the first man noticed Boyd's and the guard's unnatural attitude. The fire wasn't going, either. He looked over in the direction they were facing, and then, after staring at Jim a full ten seconds, announced, "Well, I'm damned!"

The others looked where he looked. Slowly they came to attention. One or two made covert attempts to look for their guns, and Jim let them look.

Boyd said suddenly, "If this is another bushwhack,

Wade, let's have it."

Jim only smiled. It was almost full light now, so that he could see every man. "Pull your boots on," he suggested. "I'll be here for some while."

He moved over to face them, picking Donaldson out from the others.

"I caught your guard asleep," he announced quietly. Mako looked over at the young puncher, his eyes gently reproving.

"I took a look at Bonsell's camp last night," Jim went on. "It's empty. Like to know where his crew is?" Without waiting for an answer, he told them. They were impressed, even the young men, one of whom apparently thought so little of their danger that he had slept on guard.

"Want to know where your man Cruver is?" Jim continued. "He's drunk at the Freighter's Pleasure. He went in town to bully a girl last night and got beat up for his pains."

He fell silent. Mitch Boyd cursed Cruver in measured disgust. The others just looked helpless.

"You're a sorry lot," Jim murmured. "Led by a sorry man on a sorry job. I spotted your campfire night before last two miles away. The only reason you're alive now is because Bonsell gives you credit for bein' a heap smarter than you are." He pointed to the rim. "What's to stop Bonsell from plantin' a dozen men up there and killin' you all in your sleep?" His voice was sharp, disgusted, and it cut like a whip.

Old man Reed said, "What's to prevent your doin' it yourself, now, Wade?"

Jim was not taking time to make an appeal. He didn't care what these men thought of him, just so they listened to him; and he went straight to the brutal point. "Why should I shoot you? Didn't Bonsell turn me over to Haynes to take the blame for that first raid? What do I owe Bonsell, only a slug in the back?"

"What do you owe us?" Mako Donaldson asked gently.

"Nothin'," Jim said bluntly. "But Bonsell wants you dead. And if I can fox Bonsell and keep you alive, I can make it harder for him. That's the kind of talk you want, isn't it?"

Mako Donaldson didn't answer, only regarded him thoughtfully. Jim looked around at these faces, all of them suspicious and resentful and a little angry. "What do you aim to do now?" Jim asked.

Mitch Boyd spoke up. "Wipe Bonsell out."

"How?"

"Find his crew and fight."

"You couldn't find his crew with a posse," Jim said mildly. "I tell you, they're scattered all over this country." He looked over at Mako. "What are you goin' to do, Mako? Ram around this country like a bunch of Ute squaws, leavin' a trail a kid could read, makin' camps like this camp tonight?" He paused. "You've seen a little in your time, Mako. How long do you think you'll last if you do that?"

"Not long," Mako admitted.

Jim shifted his attack. "What kind of a man do you think Bonsell is?" he inquired mildly. "What would you do if I told you that Max Bonsell was in the Excelsior house the other night when you surrounded it?"

"Then he's dead," one of the younger men said.

"He's as alive as you are," Jim said. "Hell, you can't even lick a man when you have him down. When Bonsell saw he was surrounded, he left that house. He went right through your lines. He shot a man of yours. He cut the cinches on your saddles so you couldn't ride for a half day. And then he piled all your beef up in Mimbres Canyon while you were braggin' to each other how tough you were."

"How do you know that?" Reed asked.

"I sat there not twenty yards from Cruver and watched the whole thing," Jim answered calmly. He saw the disbelief in their faces turn to sheepishness.

"I'm cold," a young puncher said. "Let's build a fire if we want to parley."

"There you got it," Jim jeered. "You're cold, so you'll build a fire, and your smoke will be spotted. In a half day, you'll have Bonsell's men swarmin' down on you." He looked contemptuously at the lot of them. "The trouble with you is, you've lived in this back lot all your lives, playin' poker together and talkin' mighty soft, on account of the whole bunch of you murdered Jim Buckner a few years back. You all know it. You all hold it over your neighbors' heads. You've never had a real fight. You can't use guns. Turn you loose in a tough Texas county and the lot of you would be swampin' out saloons because you weren't smart or tough enough to run cattle."

His voice was savage with scorn. "What kind of slick-eared dude do you take this Bonsell for? Do you know he's payin' out over two thousand dollars a month for that fightin' crew of his? I know what they are because I've seen them—a killin', cutthroat crew that could brag of a hundred murders between 'em. He didn't hire 'em for protection; he hired 'em to clean this range for him. And they're a bunch of curly wolves that can do it. They've partly done it already. And they're only waitin' for one more dumb move of yours to finish it."

Boyd blustered, "I'll fight any man in his crew and lick him."

"Nobody is questionin' your guts," Jim said quietly. "I'm questionin' your brains. I had to wake up your guard out here this mornin' so you wouldn't die of fright when you saw me in camp. You, Boyd, you were buildin' a fire. You didn't have a gun on you, did you? I could have knocked you over like a sage hen. With another man, I could have killed the lot of you in your blankets. I'm holdin' the whole lot of you now with one damn gun!"

Boyd started to protest when Mako Donaldson said curtly, "Keep quiet, Boyd!" He turned to Jim now. "What you say is true, Wade. We aren't a match for Texas fightin' men. We're small ranchers, and when we got into trouble, we turned to Cruver."

"And he's drunk now. He doesn't give a hoot for the whole lot of you."

Mako nodded. "That's right. Now we're right where we started. What should we do?"

"What do you want to do?"

"Lick Bonsell, of course."

"But you can't do it. You admit that."

Mako answered carefully, resignedly, "No, it don't look like we could."

"And you haven't got fifty head of beef between you. You haven't got houses, barns, tools, wagons, not even food. You haven't got money. You don't own the land you're on. Even if you did you couldn't hold it against Bonsell's crew. What have you got, Donaldson?"

Mako was silent.

Jim said, "What's holdin' the lot of you here? You, Mako, you've got a son. Are you goin' to stay here and let him be hunted down and killed? You, Boyd. You got two boys. Would you stack them up against an *hombre* like Ball or Pardee or MaCumber in a gun fight? You can't give 'em land when you die, nor cattle, nor a house. What can you give 'em?"

"Then you think we should pull out?" Mako said.

"If you can get out."

Boyd said, "Whaddaya mean, if we can get out?"

Patiently, Jim reiterated what he had said. Boyd might be sure that every road, old and new, every trail, even the

cattle trails, would be patrolled once a day by Bonsell's
riders. If they spotted the tracks of a dozen riders on any
of these, Bonsell's men would follow. And when a man
least expected it, he would strike.

"Then how can we get out?"

"Split up in pairs and keep to the rough country," Jim
said quickly. "Don't build fires and don't stop ridin' for
a week. Sift out of the country. Don't stop to fight, just
run."

It was brutal advice, but as Jim gave it, he looked at the
faces of these men and knew he had won. They were heart-
sick and broken already, held together by Cruver's jeering
arrogance. Without the driving temper of him, they saw
their predicament in a colder and clearer light. They were
defeated, and Mako Donaldson was the first to acknowledge it.

"I'll vote that way," he said quietly. "This is a hell of a
country, haunted for every last man of us. I've fought it
half a lifetime, and it's brought me to this. I know when
I'm licked."

Jim holstered his gun and then said nothing, but the
gesture gave an impetus to the others. Boyd was the stubborn one, but he was arguing for the sake of argument, Jim
knew. Mako took up the cudgels for Jim, and Jim squatted there, almost forgotten, as these beaten men gathered
in a loose circle around Mako and Boyd and listened to
the heat of their arguments.

The sun laid its flat light on the land now, framing long
shadows that still held the night's chill. Jim rose and
moved over into the sun, letting it warm him. He was
standing that way, back to the sun, when—

Crash!

The sharp flat explosion of a rifle blasted the morning
stillness.

Jim whirled around, took a step backward, caught himself, and drawled quietly, "You built one too many fires, boys. This is it."

Chapter Twelve: POCKET OF HELL

THE SQUATTERS LOOKED AT JIM for a long second, giving a second man on the rimrock time for a clean shot. It caught Boyd in the back and drove him to his knees and then to his face.

Jim yelled, "Your guns, dammit, your guns! Get into the brush!"

Suiting words to actions, he rolled behind a thick piñon at the edge of the camp. Mako Donaldson, swearing softly, made the tree behind him just as three more rifles joined the shooting. Jim felt his arm, and his hand came away sticky. But it was a poor shot and a clean wound. The slug had driven through the fleshy part of his upper left arm. Bandaging it swiftly with his handkerchief, he took stock of the situation. A neater death trap than this could not have been found. Sooner or later, these riflemen up on the rim would flush out down the canyon, and only a miracle would bring a man through that gantlet of fire. And Jim was not fooling himself; he was the man they wanted. He was the man they had shot at first.

The squatters were beginning to return the fire, but there was nothing to shoot at. The Excelsior slugs were searching out the trees now. Soon it would be too hot to remain here.

Bellied down, Jim peered out from under the tree at the canyon rim. It was not steep, salted with boulders which would afford some protection. A rush up it would be suicide, but not as quick suicide as a run down the canyon. Four riflemen were stationed up there, and they were doing their shooting with vicious accuracy.

Jim turned to Mako, whose seamed face held a fatalism

that he could not hide.

"Where are your horses?" Jim asked.

"The very back of the canyon. In a cave there."

"Send a man up here to me, a good man."

Mako called back through the brush. Presently, a young puncher came crawling on his belly to Jim. He was in his early twenties, a sober-faced leaned-down man whose eyes held a wild excitement.

"The rest of us have got to get out of here," Jim said, "but you're going to stay. Now listen to what I say. I've picked out four rifles up there, and there must be more, because four men wouldn't attack this crowd. They're tryin' to stampede us down the canyon, and the rest of that crew will be strung along it, waitin' to pick us off. Our one chance is to rush that rim and fort up on the ridge beyond it."

"You'll never make it," the puncher said quietly.

"Maybe not. There's a little cover here between here and the horses. We'll dash for them. Mako says there's shelter where they are. Is there?"

"Yeah. It's a cave, kind of, with an overhang of rock."

Jim nodded. "That'll give us time for my plan. But I want you to stay in the cave after we've pulled out."

"What for?"

"Because if we make that rim, we won't have a horse left under us. I'll try to make the ridge back of the rim and fort up there. When we've drawn them up surroundin' us, you make a dash down the canyon."

"For help?"

"Help, hell!" Jim said savagely. "The only help you can get is San Jon. They wouldn't be back here before midnight. By that time—"

"Yeah, I know," the puncher said. "There won't be a man alive."

Jim nodded curtly. "You've got to get horses."

"How many?"

"About eight," Jim said. "That's more'n we'll need when we finish here. I don't know how you'll get 'em. Can you do it?"

The puncher nodded.

"When you get 'em, leave them over to the west of the fight, some place where they're safe. When you've done that, you've got to come back to this cave for the saddles and bridles we'll leave. Can you do that?"

Again the puncher nodded.

"Then saddle those horses and make your way back to us on foot. If you can't get through, then build a fire on a height of land over to the south to tell us you're ready. When we see that fire, what's left of us will pull out for the horses, headin' due west of the ridge. You've got to pick us up somewhere out there in the dark and take us to the horses." He paused, watching the puncher's face. "Can you do it, mister?"

"Hell, yes," the man answered immediately.

"Then we'll rush the cave when the word's passed around." He turned back to Mako and told him to pass the word around to break for the cave. Mako did. When Jim figured that time enough had elapsed, he rose up on one knee, rammed his gun in his belt, and broke free of the brush. His course was zigzag, from shelter to shelter. A rifleman on the rim tried to search him out, but Jim didn't give him enough time to sight.

Ahead of him, he saw the wide, high opening of the cave yawning darkly in the rock. It was a huge pocket eroded by the wind, big enough to shelter a dozen horses with ease.

When Jim achieved it, he quieted the horses while the others, one by one, either made the cave or did not. He did not want to watch them, to see that grim fear on their faces, for this was only the beginning. When the last man came through safely, they made a count. There had been eleven men here. There were eight now, only one of them hit besides Jim.

In the still shelter of the cave, with only the stamping of the restless horses to interrupt him, Jim told them his plan. He laid no blame on them for the attack, since what was done was done. But he explained a simple choice—either they could saddle up and try for the canyon mouth, running the fire of a dozen guns that were certain to be there, or else they could make a daring and fast try for the ridge beyond, with only these four riflemen to harry them. They voted for the ridge at once. They listened to Jim like children, and when he saw their blind faith in him, he could hardly make himself go on.

Every man here, he announced, was to fashion a hackamore of his lariat, leaving saddles and bridles here. He himself would lead the rush for the rim. Once outside the cave, they would turn up the slope, swinging under the necks of their horses, Indian fashion. It would give them the necessary half-minute protection, if they were lucky, until they achieved the boulders, and from there on it was every man for himself in the fight for the ridge. The first men up must silence the two rifles on this side of the rim. Every man must carry all the ammunition he could, for this would be a siege.

The firing outside had stopped. The Excelsior crew could afford to hold their fire until a last futile dash for the canyon mouth took place. In case the squatters didn't come out before dark, there was dynamite to take care of that.

Mako's puncher remained dismounted. When the others had made the hackamores and mounted, bending over because of the low ceiling, Jim pulled out his gun, looked around at them, and then gave the signal, putting his spurs to his horse.

At sight of them boiling out, fire from the rim opened up again. Jim, slung under his horse's neck, put his mount up the slope. Another rider passed him and, just short of the rocks, had his horse shot down. Jim saw him fall free and make the shelter of the boulders, rock splinters whipping up around him. Jim's horse only lasted a second longer, but once he had made the rocks, he pulled up his rifle and started to throw lead at the opposite rim. Under his scorching fire, the rifleman withdrew, and the other riders had a better chance. Three of them, fighting their lunging horses up that treacherous slope, in and out of the rock maze, almost made the rim before their horses were killed. The others, afoot, advanced swiftly, the racket of their gunfire a clanging bedlam in these rocks. Jim saw they were converging on one rifleman. He chose the other, almost directly over the cave. Passing from one rock to another, he soon saw that this man had not discovered him, but was shooting over his head at the others.

With careful haste made necessary by the situation, Jim circled wide, coming up to the right of the sniper. Almost at the rock rim, he cut back toward him.

The sniper was settled in a little pocket where he could command the valley. His gun was pointed southeast. Jim approached from the north. Crouching down against the rocks, he was not ten feet from this man. To achieve the pocket, however, there was a six-foot sheer of sandstone that he had to mount.

Gun in hand, he got his wind back, then swung himself up on the scarp. The man was lying on his belly, sighting his rifle. Jim's gun butt scraped loudly on the rock, and the man whirled at the sound.

It was MaCumber. For one part of a second, he looked at Jim, and then he swiveled his gun around, shooting wide from his hip in his haste for the mark. Jim, half his body over the edge, gun in hand, thumbed back the hammer, and MaCumber's body jogged abruptly. Surprise washed into his eyes. And then Jim, hanging there, emptied his gun at him.

MaCumber went over backward. Swiftly, noting only the livid bruises and cuts on the man's face, a reminder of that night at the Star 88, Jim took his rifle and shells and ran for the ridge. The other rifleman was silenced now, but the two on the opposite rim were lacing out at them.

The ridge was flat-topped, perhaps thirty by forty feet at its peak, and was sprinkled thick with big boulders. Jim reached it first and counted the others that came over the rim and up the slope on the run.

He counted five men—Mako Donaldson and his son and three young punchers. Then no more came. They had lost three men in the canyon, two more on the slope. One man was getting horses; counting himself, there were six of them to make the fight from here on. Not a horse had lived through the storming of the rock rim.

Mako Donaldson, panting for breath, hunkered down behind a rock, while Jim took stock of their ammunition. There was enough to hold out till dark, he judged. He posted his men so that they had full command of all sides of the ridge, rearranging the smallest boulders so that they afforded protection. The ammunition was pooled in the center of the cleared space. There was a canteen which Jim had thought to bring along on his belt. Hunger would punish them, thirst, too, but they could hold out till night. If help didn't come then, it didn't matter.

Mako watched Jim with grave, tired eyes, and then Jim sat down to smoke.

"Funny," Mako said at last. "Of all of those that murdered Jim Buckner, there's only me and Will-John Cruver to tell the tale."

Young Donaldson said bitterly, "Ain't we paid for that, Dad?"

"I reckon," Mako said, content. "All but me. And I'll pay, too."

Everything was quiet now. It was a sunny morning with only a faint smell of powder in the air to give a clue to what had happened. Not a man of the Excelsior crew was in sight, but Jim knew they would come. Bonsell was out to finish his job. And with Jim Wade as his quarry, he would not stop till every man was dead.

Jim considered the situation. The slope of the river was clear of trees, and the biggest rocks which would afford a man protection had rolled down to the base of the slope. Six men could hold the place forever, given enough food and water. Maybe they'd have to, he thought calmly.

Five minutes later a rifle cracked out, and the slug ricocheted harmlessly off a boulder. Two others joined in.

"That's the beginnin'," Jim said quietly. "Don't shoot till you're sure of a man. Remember, this ammunition has got to last till dark." He smiled. "Settle down to it, boys, or this may be where you'll be buried."

Holding their fire, they watched the Excelsior riders surround the ridge. Seldom did they catch sight of a man, but only saw a swift-moving patch of his shirt, or the sun flash of a gun. There was nothing to shoot at, yet an implacable ring of riflemen was being thrown around the base of the ridge.

Presently a lone rifleman opened fire, and others slowly joined in. And Jim came to realize how well their fort had been chosen. Without bothering to return the fire, and with eyes glued to cracks in the boulders, the squatter crew waited, safe behind their wall of rock. When an Excelsior rifleman became a little too eager and showed himself, a slug would scare him back to cover. As long as daylight lasted, they were safe.

There were a dozen men shooting at them, the bulk of the Excelsior crew. But Max Bonsell was not going to waste men trying to capture a place that was impregnable in daylight. Darkness would afford him his opportunity.

The day dragged on, and by noon the rocks were warmed to an oven heat. The men sought what little shade there was and tried not to remember they were hungry and thirsty. The futile rifles hammered at them all day long, their slugs whistling harmlessly off into the blue.

Toward dark, Jim considered the situation. There was no moon tonight, which was to Bonsell's advantage. But the situation was not entirely hopeless. He marked off the rocks on top of which each man of the crew was to take his position. The same darkness that afforded Bonsell cover would allow them freedom in showing themselves. Ammunition was distributed, and then Jim outlined his scheme.

"If we're goin' to get out of here," he announced, "it's got to be tonight. And we've got to sneak through that bunch of gunnies to get to our horses. Now if we return shot for shot all through the night here, it's goin' to look suspicious when our fire drops off as we sneak out of here. But if we don't shoot much, if we let them carry the fight to us and hold our fire till the last minute, they'll sort of get used to our not firin'. There'll be long waits, minutes at a time when we don't shoot a gun. We've got to get 'em used to that. Once that's done, they won't think it's funny when we stop shootin' to leave."

When full dark came, they took up their positions on top of their rocks. They were much more exposed here, in danger of sky-lining themselves for targets, but it was necessary risk. Jim argued them out of smoking at all, since their eyes, once keyed to the darkness, would be blinded by any match flare.

And they waited, their guns silent. A desultory fire was kept up by the Excelsior outfit. More than anything else, Jim wanted to bait Bonsell into thinking their ammunition was exhausted.

It was a strain, peering down into that darkness where everything was a slight variation of gray. A man's nerves started to crawl, and he would jump at the merest sound.

Two full hours after dark, however, they were rewarded. Jim was watching on the side sloping into the canyon, simply because this was the side on which an attack would be least expected. For minutes now, he had been watching a shape down the slope that was just a little darker than the night. He thought he saw it move.

Then faintly there came to him the clink of a spur on rock.

When he was sure it was a man, or many men, he whispered to Mako, "They're sneakin' up my side."

"Want help?"

"No. Stay where you are. Pass the word around. It may be a trick to get us all over on this side. Just forget about me and watch your own territory."

The rifles below kept hammering away—and the dark blot grew larger on the slope. Jim watched it grimly, not moving. He was beginning to make out shapes now, but he made no move to raise his rifle. He didn't want to make a mistake now.

At last, however, he could distinctly make out the forms of the attackers. They were more than halfway up the slope, just beginning to fan out.

He picked out the leader, took careful aim, and fired. He saw the man go down, heard his rifle clatter on the rock. The others fell on their faces, trying to hide. But Jim turned upon them, lacing shots low, so that rock splinters were kicked up in their faces. It was all over in a minute. Jim heard one of them call something, then there came a pounding of footsteps and the sliding of rock. He raked the slope with swift shots, and then all was silent again.

Immediately, Bonsell tried another plan. It was the old Indian way of fighting, taking advantage of each piece of cover, and carrying a running fight up the hill. Evidently, his men were set for it, for as soon as the first attackers were driven back, the second wave started.

This was more effective. Instead of stealth being used, this swift charge was designed to overwhelm them. A defender could only settle on one attacker, and while he was throwing shots at him, three others would advance up the hill, heckle him into turning his attention to them, while the first man advanced farther.

A kind of panic seized the squatters. Jim could tell by the number of their shots that they weren't aiming, rather shooting out of desperation. There were no men climbing his side of the slope, but he did not crawl over to join the others. He dropped down to the floor of the ridge, put his shoulder to the smallest boulders, and teetered them over the edge.

It was a terrifying noise in the dark. The hollow booming thunder of their descent gained in volume as they picked up speed, until the ground shook. Then a crash among the trees, and a prolonged ripping of smashed brush and broken trees rose to join the noise of the gunfire.

The Excelsior crew didn't mind the gunfire. They could tell where their enemy was by the spot of his gun flash. But rocks were different. You could hear them, but you couldn't see them, and every one sounded as if it was headed for you.

Jim worked violently, pushing whatever rocks he could find, taking no aim. He calculated on the sound and their invisibility to spread a terror through these men that guns could not.

And he was lucky. He rolled one large one over the side, then turned to hunt another. He had barely found it when he heard a man's agonized scream rise over the clatter. It lifted in a long, piercing wail, trailing for three seconds in the night, and then it ceased abruptly. It sent a shiver down his spine.

And then the fire from the slope slacked off. He heard a man cursing wildly down at the base of the ridge. That would be Bonsell, taunting his men, driving them forward.

But they were cowed. Slowly, their gun flashes receded down the slope, showing less often as the Excelsior crew, afraid to make a target for a boulder, held their fire.

Jim watched breathlessly, and heard old Mako Donaldson chuckling. And then he lifted his glance, attracted by a dim point of light far to the south. As he watched, he saw a small fire flare up, burn for seconds, then die.

There was the puncher with their horses.

Jim, seizing the moment, gave swift orders to his men. "Get down here and roll rocks—every one you can find! Gang up on them; get some big ones rolling down every side!"

As they worked, he told them of seeing the fire. "We'll drive these gunnies so far back in the brush, they won't come out for an hour."

He put his good shoulder against a big boulder and the others threw their weight beside him. The rock teetered, settled back, teetered again, and went over. The noise was monstrous. It went crashing down the slope in long, shattering leaps, a trail of sparks marking each place it hit. A wild yell, "Look out!" arose from the base of the ridge, and then the rock hit the first tree. It broke it off with the sound of rifleshot, and then plunged on. Tree after tree went down before its thunder, and for a full half minute afterward they could hear it smash its terrible course until momentum was gone.

Then they set to work with a will. There were no answering gunshots now. No man down there wanted to offer the flash of his gun as a target for a boulder.

When they had moved every boulder that was movable, Jim gave swift directions.

"Cut off down the west slope. Every boulder we find on the way, we'll push down. Come on, and quick about it!"

Max Bonsell's shout had come from the south side of the ridge. Jim felt certain that he had been forced to withdraw his men straight back out of range of the rocks, rather than order them to dodge. They made their silent way down the west slope now, shoving whatever boulders came in their path. There was no gunfire, not a sound except the rolling, leaping rumble of the boulders.

Once at the base of the hill, screened by the piñons and cedars, the six of them marched swiftly in Indian file, and ducked into the first arroyo they found. Its sand cushioned their footsteps. After they had walked for what Jim judged was five minutes, they rested, and sought a height of land. Once there, he sat down to wait.

Presently another small fire showed up for a moment straight ahead of them, and died almost as suddenly. But it was enough.

Fifteen minutes later, a voice softly hailed them. It was the puncher.

"The horses are waitin' just over the ridge," he announced.

There were eight horses. There were seven men to ride them. Jim hadn't calculated badly.

When it came time to mount, Jim gave them the last bit of advice he was ever to give them.

"In your place, I'd hit for the mountains, and never stop ridin' till I was through them. Once through, I'd scatter."

"To where?" Mako Donaldson murmured.

Jim didn't answer, for he knew how a country, however hostile and bitter, can grow into a man, become part of him. And this was the last time these men would ever see this range, or ever claim it for home.

Mako stepped into the saddle and regarded Jim musingly.

"And you, Wade," he said, "what's left for you?"

"I'll stick," Jim said. "I've got a score to settle. I'll settle it for you, too."

"It strikes me we wouldn't be here to ride if it wasn't for you," Mako said, and Jim made a deprecatory gesture that went unseen in the dark.

"I'm an old man," Mako said. "I don't like to die in debt to a man. But I reckon I'll have to." He put out his hand, and Jim shook it. "Thanks, friend," Mako said.

Jim shook hands all around. None of these men, close-mouthed and inarticulate, tried to thank him. It was understood, and that's the way he wanted to have it.

When they were gone, he listened until the last sound of their retreat gave way to the dim rattle of gunfire in the east. Bonsell was making another attack, and this time he would carry the ridge—to find it empty. It was time to ride.

He mounted wearily and headed for San Jon. He had partly corrected a mistake that would have ridden his every waking hour the rest of his life, he thought.

Chapter Thirteen: FORGED CORNERS

SCOVILLE WAS MENDING A BRIDLE, sitting out on the back steps of Lily's house and letting the sun warm him. He was whistling softly, a token of a good breakfast just finished and peace in his heart.

He saw a man ride up the alley, turn, and pause at the rear of the blacksmith shop. Scoville didn't know him, and he regarded him idly as the man leaned over the horn of his saddle and exchanged words with Tom Beauchamp. He saw Tom gesture toward the house. The man dismounted, left his horse, and approached the house with a saddle-stiff, rolling gait that told of many hours in the saddle.

When he was close, Scoville nodded civilly. "Howdy."

The man didn't answer. He had a narrow head, clamped on his neck by the squarest jaw Scoville had ever seen. The blond beard-stubble on his cheeks couldn't soften the line of that jaw, and his close-set eyes announced to the world that he didn't give a damn whether anyone liked the set of his jaw or not.

"I come from Cope's saloon," he said meagerly. "They told me I'd find a man by the name of Peters lives here."

Peters! That was the name with which Cope had signed his letter to Buckner! Scoville looked up at the man, and he didn't like him, didn't like anything about him, not even the suggestively low set of the twin guns on his thighs.

"Yeah? Maybe he does," he answered.

"You Peters?"

"What if I am?"

The man looked about him and then said one word in a lowered voice. "Buckner."

Scoville spat carefully. "I'd heard it rumored that Buckner was a fine figure of a man. And if you're a fine figure of a man, cowboy, then my taste runs to women."

The man's eyes veiled over. "I'm not Buckner."

"That's what I think. I was just tryin' to tell you."

"Buckner's outside of town, down in the bottoms."

"That's fine," Scoville said.

"He'd like to talk to you."

"What's stoppin' him? You know where I am, don't you?"

The man's feet shifted faintly, his impatience mounting. "If you'd get on a horse, we'd be out there in ten minutes."

Scoville spat again. "You've forgot somethin', haven't you?"

"Like what?"

"Like money. You know—what you get drunk with,

what you buy horses with, what puts fat in the head, like yours."

The man still held his temper. "If you want money, talk to Buckner."

Scoville leaned his elbows on the step above him and turned his face up to the man. "What's your name, mister?"

"Warren. Ray Warren."

"Well, Ray Warren," Scoville drawled, "you look like a man that's seen the elephant and hear'n the owl hoot. You must have been in a store, once in your life, anyway. You know in a store you buy somethin' and give the man money for it. It's a custom."

Warren said, "I told you Buckner will talk about that when we get out there."

"That's just it," Scoville said. "Did you ever see a storekeeper follow a customer home, then set down and talk about the price of what he wants to buy? You see, I'm the storekeeper in this case. You're the customer. You come to me—with money."

"How much?"

"A couple of hundred to start with."

"I ain't got it."

"Go get it. I don't sell to broke people."

Warren regarded Scoville a long moment, a look of cold disgust on his face. "Ever hear of a customer tellin' a storekeeper what he thought of highway robbery over a counter?" he asked softly.

"Can't say I have."

"I heard one threaten to beat hell out of a storekeeper once, just because he didn't like the way he talked."

"And I saw a storekeeper take a customer apart once, just to see what caused that loud noise inside him. Know what it was? It was just a lot of hot air that smelled like a skunk and barked like a coyote and had a long woolly tail ucked under its legs, like a sheep."

Warren's face didn't change. "I'll be back," he said.

"Oh, don't bother comin' if it's any trouble," Scoville
aid innocently. "I won't miss you."

When Warren had gone, Scoville's face relaxed into a
rin. He heard a noise behind him and glanced up at the
loor. Lily was standing just inside it, her eyes dancing
vith laughter.

"Did anybody ever tell you," she said, laughing, "that
our manners in public aren't much different from a ter-
ier dog's?"

Scoville grinned and said, "No, ma'am," and Lily came
ut to sit with him.

"You see," Scoville drawled, "for nearly a week now, me
nd Ben have been sweatin' out there on the grant. We've
urned charcoal and buried it for them fake corner mark-
rs. We've dug up the old corners and smoothed 'em out
nd toted those stone markers over to put in the new char-
oal. We've sweat and got plenty dirty and cussed and ate
old grub and rode until I near to wore my saddle out. I
eckon we're due for a little fun, so I might's well have it
vith this jughead."

"He looked like a rough customer," Lily said, a little
vorry creeping into her eyes.

"Yeah," Scoville said carelessly. "Every time I see one of
hem steely-eyed gunnies walkin' around on his hind legs
vith a I-dare-you-to-do-it look in his eyes, I just can't help
wistin' his tail."

"Be careful, Phil," Lily said suddenly. "If he works for
Buckner, we can be sure he's just as crooked as his boss.
After he's got the information from you that he wants,
ie'll probably turn on you and pistol-whip you."

Scoville looked at her, his eyes surprised and hurt. "Pis-
ol-whip me? That stuffed Stetson? Why, lady, I'll tie him
n a knot and pin him on your hat, if you give the word."

Lily looked fondly at him. She understood that beneath his levity there was a real contempt for men like Warren, and that these men stirred up a fearless hatred in him. Moreover, he was a better man than they were, as his handling of Cruver proved. Other times, his real gentleness showed.

Warren returned in a half hour, and Scoville was still mending his bridle.

At sight of Warren, Scoville grinned. "If he trusted you with two hundred bucks out of his sight, he's a bigger sucker than you are for not runnin' away with it."

Warren unsmilingly handed him a stack of gold pieces. Scoville pocketed them and went out and saddled his horse.

Buckner's camp was down-river, a couple of miles off the stage road.

Scoville sized up the man before he dismounted among the cottonwoods. Buckner was an impressive-looking man, and not all his impressiveness stemmed from his rich black suit, now covered with dust, and his fine hand-tooled boots. He had a thin and sensitive face, untanned by wind or weather, and his hair was white and thick. *This was what Mary Buckner's father looked like,* Scoville thought. Only the man who sired Mary would have had eyes not quite so calculating, and his chin would have been a little firmer. Also, he would not have had that arrogant, impatient cast to his face, or if he had, he would have apologized for it with a smile. Harvey Buckner did no such thing.

He said, "You're Peters?"

Scoville got down. "Sometimes," he drawled. "Sometimes not. It depends on who I'm talkin' to."

"Are you the man who wrote me about Bonsell?"

Scoville wanted to be cross-grained. He was going to enjoy this. "Depends on who you are," he said. "I didn't catch the name."

Buckner looked faintly irritated. "Buckner, of course. ames Buckner." He held up the letter. "Answer my ques-on. Are you the man who wrote me this letter?"

"Depends," Scoville said. "I ain't seen the letter yet."

Buckner walked over and handed him the letter. Sco-ille looked at it and said, "I might have."

"Well, I've paid you good money for information. I ant that information."

"You only paid me a little less than half. It'll cost you nother three hundred to get what you want."

Buckner looked over at Warren, who shrugged. Then, ithout protest, he opened his shirt to disclose a money elt. He took it off and dumped its contents on a blanket, hich flanked a cold fire. From the pile of gold coins, he ounted out another three hundred dollars in gold eagles nd passed them over to Scoville.

Scoville, unwilling to pass up the chance to tender an nsult, picked three coins at random, tested them with his eeth, and then pocketed them.

"All right. What do you want to know?"

"You said Bonsell had changed the boundaries of the Jlibarri grant. Is that true?"

"Yes."

"How do you know?"

"Because I done the work myself."

Buckner's eyes narrowed. "How did you do it?"

"Buried charcoal in a pit and put the old stone in the iddle of it, like the old corners was fixed."

"You mean it looks like the old corner?"

"As near as I could make it."

Buckner was quiet a moment. "How much land was aken off?"

"Along the west boundary, I reckon it was close to ten iles. Same on the north."

Buckner looked at him shrewdly. "You're lying, Peters."

"All right, I'm lying."

"Aren't you?"

"That's what you said. You ought to know. Of course, a man with brains might think of havin' me show him."

"I intend to do that," Buckner said absently. "But on the face of it, it sounds like a lie. Bonsell wouldn't dare do such a thing. How could he get away with it?"

"You ever see the old markers?" Scoville countered.

"No."

"Then if you never saw the old markers, how would you know that they'd been changed?"

"Why, the records, of course."

"All right. But when a man has that much land, he just takes it for granted. He don't run to check the corners. He just asks his foreman to show him. An estimate is good enough."

"Not for me."

"No, he didn't figure it would be good enough for you," Scoville said. "Bonsell said you'd suspect your own mother of givin' you lead quarters for the Sunday-school collection."

Buckner flushed. "He did, did he? Well, what's to stop me from prosecuting him?"

"Blackmail," Scoville said mildly.

It gave him a feeling of pleasure to see the caution creep into Buckner's eyes. "Blackmail?" he echoed. "What kind of blackmail?"

"He never said. Only he told us if you got salty about it, he always had somethin' he could threaten you with." That threat, Scoville thought, being his real identity.

Buckner considered this a long moment, and Scoville could almost see him weighing his chances. Could Max Bonsell gather definite proof that he was not James Buckner? The answer was no, Bonsell couldn't, and it showed in the confident smile Buckner displayed.

"Now, my man, come along," he said in a businesslike way. "I want to see the forged corners."

"It'll take a day's ride."

"Of course it will! Are you ready to ride?"

All that day they rode west, since San Jon was located just over the middle of the south boundary. It was a strange ride, one in which Scoville had a chance to gauge the mettle of Buckner. He found him a closemouthed man, not disposed to talk of his own affairs. On the other hand, he wanted to know the affairs of the Excelsior. He was amazed to hear that it had been burned down, but he received the news of the destruction of the squatters' cattle with obvious pleasure. Of the fight on the ridge and the flight of the squatters, he knew nothing simply because Scoville did not know of it himself.

They camped at dark "close to the corner," as Scoville put it, and Scoville slept peacefully, since he would be of use to them until they knew the exact location.

Next morning, bright and early, Scoville lead them to the corner marker. It lay atop the tallest ridge in sight. A great deal of work had been put in here by Ben and himself. Trees had been grubbed out by their roots, until the ridge was absolutely bald. Four tall cairns had been built, and in the center of them was yet a taller one. Under this lay the charcoal, and buried in it was the marker of soft sandstone, inscribed in Spanish after the corrective survey in the early 1800's.

Buckner looked at it and remarked, "This is certainly fresh-looking. Not much attempt to disguise it."

"One good rain and it would look a hundred years old," Scoville said. "Just wash the dirt away and give that pile of brush time enough to dry out so it'll burn. If you'd waited a month longer, you couldn't have told it from the old one."

"And where is it?"

"Over that next line of hills."

Scoville pulled out his sack of tobacco and rolled a smoke, waiting for what was coming. Buckner looked at the ground carefully.

"This is skillful up to a point," he said. "As I remember it, the record of the original survey says that on the southwest corner, the marker lies on a butte, whose south face is of black *malpais*. I don't see any *malpais*."

Scoville shook his head. "No, you're wrong. It says a butte of white quartz formation in the survey records. This may be a little over ten miles from the real marker, but it's the only butte of white quartz formation we could find around here. That's why we picked it."

Buckner looked up swiftly. "No, my man, *you're* wrong. It says a butte with a black face. Have you seen the survey records?"

"Hunh-unh. But Bonsell has, hasn't he?"

Buckner nodded. "But he's got it wrong if he says it speaks of a butte of white quartz."

Scoville took the cigarette from his face and laughed. "If I had to bet between your memory and Bonsell's, I'd bet on Bonsell's. He never forgot a place he ever saw, a face he ever saw, or a name he ever read. And I can't be mistaken because he picked this place out himself. The translation said, 'From this butte of white quartz, a line was run ninety miles due east to—' "

"Eighty miles," Buckner prompted.

"Ninety miles."

"Eighty miles! Good God! Whose land is this, yours or mine?"

"Listen," Scoville said sharply. "I ain't feeble-minded. I'm repeatin' what Bonsell said—and he said that. You got a charter for this land, ain't you?"

"Yes."

"Can you read Spanish?"

"Of course."

"So can Bonsell. He can speak it. And Bonsell said that charter translated meant that the grant was ninety by forty miles."

Buckner looked at him in open amazement. "You mean Bonsell told you that?"

"I said it, didn't I?"

"But translated it says eighty miles, not ninety miles."

"You got it with you?" Scoville countered. "I know Spanish."

"You fool, do you think I carry it with me?"

"I dunno. That's what I asked."

"I don't," he said. "But I can find out when I get back to town." He looked around him again, smiling. "Well, this butte business will prove a forgery. Bonsell got a look at those survey reports along with the charter one night. Apparently his memory isn't as good as you suppose."

Scoville shrugged indifferently, willing to let the matter drop. He had done what Jim Wade asked him to do, and that was to try and find out if Harvey Buckner had the charter with him. He did have, but just where, Scoville didn't know.

Buckner turned to Scoville. "What did you say your real name was?"

Scoville's hand dropped to his gun. He whipped it up before Ray Warren could make a move.

"Scoville," he said. "You can tell that to Bonsell if you want. Just in case he denies it. Watch him when you give the name." He waited.

"What's the gun for?" Buckner asked.

"I'm just careful," Scoville murmured. "I've got five hundred dollars on me. That curly wolf that rides with you would kill a man for white cigarette papers if he decided he didn't like to smoke brown ones. I'm lightin' a shuck. Anything else you'd like to know?"

Buckner smiled. "Nothing, thank you."

"You're good and damn welcome," Scoville said. "If I can prove to you that Bonsell's a crook and has been cheatin' you, it's worth a heap more than the gold you gave me. So long."

Backing away, he led his horse down the slope and into the brush and rode off. Neither Warren nor Buckner made any attempt to follow him. He wondered if Buckner believed all this of Bonsell, and judged that he did. That done, there was only one thing remaining. He must try to find out where Buckner had the charter.

He waited until he judged the two of them had left, then swung back and picked up their trail. They were headed for town, riding at a long mile-eating trot, backtracking themselves. Every so often, on a height of land, he would pull up and glass the country. Ahead, not more than a mile, Buckner and Warren were riding east.

Scoville settled down to following them. In midmorning, he saw where their tracks split, one heading north, toward the hill hide-out where Scoville told Buckner Bonsell's crew was holed up, the other heading for San Jon. On the next ridge, Scoville saw that it was Buckner who was riding for town and at a faster pace than formerly.

Once Scoville was sure of Buckner's destination, he circled out and, alternating between a walk and a trot, struck out for town. It was a steady, mile-eating pace, and he knew that he would reach San Jon before Buckner.

Presently he struck the San Jon road, and just outside of town he stopped and pulled his horse back in the brush and watched the road.

In fifteen minutes Buckner rode by. Following at a safe distance, Scoville saw him ride into the plaza and pull up at the tie rail in front of the bank. He went inside, was there ten minutes, then came out. He walked over to

Kling's emporium, came out with a package, got his horse, put him up at the feed stable, and then went over to the hotel, just as the town was lighting up for dark.

Scoville tried to piece all these moves together and decided he couldn't unless he knew one thing. He went into the bank and asked a clerk, "Did a big tall gent with a lantern jaw leave some papers here yesterday to be called for by another man, by that gent that just went out?"

The clerk said, "We aren't allowed to give out that information."

"I know. I don't care about the papers. I just think I recognized him. Might be by the name of Warren?"

The clerk relented and said he thought that was the man's name.

Scoville left, grinning. A little guessing might tell a man that the first thing Warren had done yesterday was to take the charter and other papers and ride in to the bank to put them in safekeeping for Buckner, who did not want his visit made public until he had talked with Scoville. That was borne out by the fact that Buckner had camped out last night, away from the town, whereas he was staying in the hotel tonight. His trip to the bank was to verify the survey words and the charter. His trip to the store was probably for a clean shirt. He had no baggage, no place else to hide the papers, or he would have carried them with him. And he would not carry them with him because it was too dangerous.

Scoville smiled a little as he waited for clean dark. Then he could tell Mary and Cope and Jim Wade something that would please them, please them mightily.

Chapter Fourteen: PLAYED FOR A SUCKER

BONSELL'S CAMP WAS in the dip between two ridges far off to the west of where the Excelsior buildings had stood. It was a shallow bowl, deep enough to afford shelter and to hide the sight of the fire, but it was a place commanding all the country surrounding. An easy place to defend, an easy place to escape from, a good hiding-place because a rider traveling either side of this ridge would not suspect there was a depression atop it capable of holding a dozen men and their horses.

His guards were numerous, and they stayed awake. One of them had spotted Ray Warren in early afternoon and had watched him try four different ridges in his attempt to find the camp. When dark came, the guard stepped out, hunted Warren down, and, at the point of a gun, asked him his business. Warren told him, and was taken back to camp.

He left his horse outside the circle of firelight and picked his way through the lounging Excelsior crew to the fire, over which Bonsell was squatting.

Bonsell looked up at his approach and, seeing him, smiled. He knew Warren well enough to distrust him, simply because the man was utterly loyal to Harvey Buckner.

They shook hands, and Bonsell said, "Didn't know you were in the country, Ray. How's the boss?"

"He's here, too. At the hotel in San Jon."

Bonsell's eyes grew wary. Funny Buckner didn't tell him about his visit, he thought. But he only said, "Good. I got a present for him."

"What's that?"

"This range is clean, now. We run the last of them squatters off last night."

"He'll be glad to hear that," Warren said. "He wants you to ride in tomorrow for a talk."

"Anything wrong?"

"I dunno. Just reckon he wants to straighten a few things up."

Bonsell nodded carelessly. "Eaten anything today?"

"Damn little."

Bonsell got up and went over to the grub box. A quarter of beef wrapped in a tow-sack hung from a branch of a tree beside the box. He took it down, slapped his pockets, then called idly, "Who's got a knife?"

Ball had one. He came over and tendered it to Bonsell, then held the quarter while Bonsell sliced off some steaks.

While he was bent over his work, Bonsell murmured, "Ball, if you can hear me clear your throat."

Ball cleared his throat.

"Go out and lame Warren's horse. Pull a shoe. *Sabe?*"

Again Ball cleared his throat. With his steaks and some cold biscuits, Bonsell went back to the fire. Warren was still warming his hands, talking with Pardee. Bonsell joined in the conversation as he prepared a meal of steaks, biscuits, and coffee, and afterward Warren ate. They talked of the fight the squatters had put up, and marveled at what stubborn men they were. Bonsell obliquely tried to question Warren as to the reasons for Buckner's visit, but Warren wasn't telling anything. His secrecy only verified what Bonsell had suspected; there was something Buckner had on his chest. And he was going to get to Buckner alone when he didn't have that gunnie of a Warren to side him.

After they had smoked, Warren rose and said, "I'll be gettin' back to town."

Bonsell politely invited him to throw his blankets here, and Warren just as politely refused.

"Then see you tomorrow in San Jon," Bonsell said.

Warren talked a moment with some of the crew, then walked over to his horse, mounted, waved, and rode off.

As soon as he was out of sight, Bonsell said to Pardee, "Saddle my black and be quick about it."

Pardee looked at him shrewdly. "You want to get Warren?"

"No," Bonsell said irritably. "Don't be a damn fool, Pardee! Nobody's to touch him. Go saddle my horse."

When the big black gelding was saddled, Bonsell mounted, left the crew in command of Ball, and disappeared into the night. He had a long ride ahead of him, and he did not spare his horse. He was going to see Buckner tonight, and about what he had no idea. But he did have an idea that something was wrong. This secret visit was not like Buckner unless he had something on his mind. Warren would lame his horse since Ball had pulled a shoe, and would not reach San Jon till daylight.

When he rode into San Jon, it was two in the morning. Instead of leaving his horse in front of the hotel at the tie rack, Bonsell pulled into the darkness of the alley and tied him beside Tom Beauchamp's blacksmith shop. Then he surveyed the back of the hotel. It was pitch-dark. Already he had decided not to advertise his visit.

He tried the hotel's kitchen door and found it was locked. Then, very quietly, he hunted about for something to stand on and finally moved the barrel from under the eave spout at the corner. Standing on it, he tried three windows at the back of the hotel, and found them locked. But he was a persistent man. The fourth one he tried on the south side was open, and he swung up into the kitchen, shutting the window softly after him. The kitchen was dark, and he moved slowly enough toward the far wall that he did not even kick a bucket of wash water which the swamper had set in the middle of the floor in readiness for his morning's scrubbing.

He found that one door in the kitchen led out into a corridor which ran the length of the building and opened onto the lobby, where a light was burning.

Softly he walked the length of the corridor, approaching the lobby with infinite care. He heard a paper rustle now and then, and when he looked around the newel post of the stairs which ascended to the second floor, he could see the night clerk seated in one of the lobby chairs reading a paper, the lamp on a table beside him. It was a young fellow whom the proprietor had hired to protect himself from the occasional freighters who demanded a room at all hours of the night.

Bonsell considered the situation. He could slug the clerk on the head, but he didn't want to leave a trail. Also, he could try to sneak up the stairs. But he was leery of the boards whose squeaks would be sure to give him away. He stood there motionless, his crafty face musing.

The lobby desk was a right-angled counter just to the right of the stairs, and on it was the register and a pen. Bonsell's glance settled on the pen, which was stuck upright in a glass of buckshot, and then his glance rose to the open double doors of the dining-room beyond the clerk.

Gently, then, he hunkered down and crept the ten feet to the counter and paused. The clerk turned a page of his paper. Bonsell's hand reached up, fumbled for the glass of buckshot, found it, and took it. In another moment he was back in his old place, and the clerk had not moved.

The rest was simple enough. Taking two buckshot in his fingers, Bonsell tossed them over the table where the lamp sat, over the clerk's head so that they landed in the door of the dining-room and rolled noisily across the floor.

At the first one, the clerk swiveled his head to listen. Two more landed and rolled off in the dark. They made a strange sound, something like a board cracking, something like a mouse skittering across paper. At the third one, the clerk put down his paper and walked over to the door and listened. No sound come from the dining-room and he came back to his paper. When he was seated again, Bonsell threw another one. This time the clerk put down his paper, picked up the lamp, and entered the dining-room. He paused in the doorway, then, as if he wanted no more worry about the noise, moved inside to investigate.

Bonsell laid the glass of shot on the desk, tucked the register under his arm, and ascended the stairs softly. Once at the head of the stair well, he waited until he heard the clerk take his seat again and resume his reading, then he tiptoed down to the far end of the corridor and around the L in it. He struck a match, consulted the register, found that he was only five doors from Buckner's room, approached it, and knocked softly on the door.

Buckner appeared in a moment, a pair of pants pulled over his nightshirt.

Bonsell smiled and murmured, "Howdy, Buckner. Warren said you wanted to see me."

Buckner smiled uneasily and extended his hand, then invited Bonsell into his room. Shutting the door behind him, he asked, "Where is Ray?"

"Puttin' up the horses. I figured I might's well ride in with him tonight."

Buckner looked relieved. "Take a chair," he said, without much warmth. He turned the lamp higher, put his coat on against the chill, and lighted a cigar. Bonsell watched him carefully. There was something wrong, and he might as well find out now what it was.

"Any trouble come up?" he asked Buckner, then smiled again. "Whatever it is, it ain't enough to make you feel bad about the news I got for you."

"And what's that?"

"The squatters are cleaned out. Last night we cornered 'em, killed six, and the rest have drifted out of the country."

Buckner regarded him with a slow smile. "That's fine, Max. You've settled all my affairs for me before we part company, haven't you?" He sat down on the bed, watching Bonsell.

Bonsell said, "Before we what?"

"Part company. You and I are through, Max."

Bonsell drawled patiently, "Now what brought that about?"

"I took a little trip today—yesterday," Buckner said. "I saw your new corners. A pretty job, but I spotted them a little too soon."

Bonsell looked blank. "What new corners?"

Buckner laughed. "You're a good actor, Max. I always said you were. But this time I've got the goods on you."

"What in hell are you talkin' about?" Bonsell drawled.

Buckner was smiling. "Just to show you how much I know about it, I can tell you the whole scheme," Buckner said. "You thought you could steal a nice slice of land from the grant by changing the corners. Chances were I'd never discover it, but if I did you figured I'd have to keep my mouth shut because I didn't want anybody snooping into my title to the grant. Well, mister, you're wrong. I spotted the steal. I saw the new corner some ten miles this side of the old one. I even talked to one of the crew that changed it under your orders. You made the blunder of misreading the survey records as to the south corner. You've located the false corner on a butte of white quartz, whereas the survey record states that it's on a butte whose south face is of black *malpais*." He smiled complacently. "For a minute I was stumped. But I made the bank before it closed and consulted the survey report. Also, you informed your man wrong as to the length of that south boundary, in case it's any interest to you. It's eighty miles, not ninety. I took a look at the old charter to make sure this afternoon."

He spread his hands. "You're a sharp man, friend Bonsell. You're so sharp you've cut your own throat."

Bonsell was trying to make sense out of this and he could not. He started at the beginning. "You think I changed boundary corners on you?"

"I know you did."

"And you saw the false corner?"

"I did."

"How'd you find it?"

"One of your crew took me."

"And who was it?"

Buckner hesitated. Scoville had said he was leaving the country, so it didn't matter if he was named. "Man by the name of Scoville," he said carefully. "Ever hear of him?"

Bonsell's face betrayed the fact that he had. "Yeah," he said. "He ran out on me when the goin' got too hot. He showed you the corner, eh? What did he tell you?"

"That he'd done it himself under your direction. You were planning to steal part of the grant and blackmail me into keeping silent about it."

Bonsell's thoughts were far ahead of him. So that rat Scoville had built this frame-up? He didn't believe it. Scoville had nothing against him. There was only one man in this country who hated him enough to do this. And that man was Jim Wade.

"Scoville," he murmured. "Did he wear a beard?"

"No."

"How'd you run across him?" Bonsell asked, surer than ever that Scoville was Wade.

Buckner smiled. "He wrote me a letter. I picked him up here in town."

"Where?"

"That house by the blacksmith shop, if that's any use to you."

That would be Lily Beauchamp's place. Jim Wade and Lily Beauchamp! Of course. They'd met and become friends the night Wade blew in. Then this was Wade's frame-up. Slow fury boiled inside Bonsell, but he glanced lazily at Buckner. Buckner was already convinced of his guilt, and there seemed no way to destroy this conviction.

To blame it on a disgruntled employee, Jim Wade, whom he could not catch, would be a feeble alibi and one Buckner would not believe. Denial of it was useless, but he might as well try it. So he said, "Did it ever occur to you, Buckner, that somebody is trying to frame me?"

"Who?"

Buckner had him there. He couldn't say, "A man I fired," and be believed. But he would have to make a stab at it. "Why, Mary Buckner, I reckon. She's the one that wants to sink us both."

Buckner smiled unpleasantly. "That's another thing I've got to thank you for. Why didn't you tell me she was here, had taken a room in this hotel about four doors down the corridor?"

"I wrote and told you. You must have left too soon to get the letter."

Buckner said with heavy sarcasm, "It makes a nice story, Max. So she's trying to frame you? You think she hired Scoville? You think she just picked him up—maybe saw him as she was riding past in the stage and called to the driver to stop. Maybe she said, 'My good man, will you guarantee to do a frame-up for me? I don't know you, but you have an honest face. And you look like you work for Max Bonsell, although I never saw him. Will you frame him for me?' Bah!" Buckner snorted. "You're guilty as hell, Max! You used to be a fair liar but you're slipping. You haven't even got a decent alibi."

Bonsell smiled thinly. "That ought to convince you I'm innocent."

"No," Buckner said. "It'd take more than that, Max. I've always known you for what you are—a killer with brains. I've used you as far as I'm able. If you'd played square with me, we'd have gone places. But I've always had a hunch that if I gave you enough rope, you'd hang yourself. You have."

Bonsell leaned forward and said quietly, "Not quite. You seem to forget that little paper we signed when we started on this deal. I was to get fifty percent of the split— in land, cattle, money, whatever we got out of it." He smiled unpleasantly. "You'd like to buy that back, wouldn't you, my friend? You can fire me and hire another man in my place, but I still get half the kitty."

Buckner threw back his head and laughed. He laughed immoderately, and Bonsell regarded him with a growing feeling of uneasiness.

"Wait a minute," Buckner said when he was through laughing. "Do you admit you're guilty of falsifying those corners?"

"I'm not," Bonsell said. "But just to make things smoother, I will."

"Good. That brings us down to the partnership contract," Buckner said. "There were two sets of papers, exactly alike. They said that we agreed to split fifty-fifty on whatever we got out of this. They said that in case of the death of one of us, the other was to receive his share. Wasn't that it?"

"It was."

Buckner said dryly, "Max, do you think I'm such a fool that I'd put my hand to an agreement like that? Do you think I would, knowing that all you'd have to do to get the whole Ulibarri grant would be to put a slug in my back? Do you?"

"I don't think," Bonsell said. "I saw you do it."

"Have you ever consulted that contract?"

"No. It's in Sante Fe in the bank."

"You ought to read it sometime," Buckner said with a smile. "There are several things that are made very clear. One of them is that in the event of my death, the incomes from the Ulibarri grant go to charity. You aren't even mentioned, my friend."

Bonsell's eyes opened. "Why, your contract was the same as mine!"

"So you thought, my friend, so you thought. But you didn't take the trouble to make sure. My lawyer handed you a contract. You read it and said it was satisfactory. My lawyer said that being so, he'd get the other contract. He took yours, turned to his portfolio, drew out the other contract, substituted the one you'd just read for it, and let you read the same one. Then he spread both on the desk and we signed, and you took the original sheet. You took the one I wanted you to take, the one leaving you out in the rain. I took the one I wanted. Therefore, the contract I have declares that if you die all your money goes to me. The one you have says that if I die, all my money goes to charity."

He smiled a little. "My friend, out here in the West it doesn't seem to be the custom to read things you sign. You trust a man. But I came from the East, where lawyers are a little sharper than these homespun orators of yours." He put his cigar out and settled back on the bed.

"You see, you haven't a share in anything. You haven't anything to gain by killing me. I think you have a phrase for it here. You are holding the sack, friend Bonsell."

Bonsell's eyes were dreamy. He should have been angry, raging; he only felt a little childish. That a shifty-eyed, smooth-talking lawyer had fooled him out of a good part of a fortune was a hard thing to take, but Bonsell was a fatalist. He didn't even doubt that every word of it was true. He had worked like a slave, risked his life a hundred times, just so he could turn over the Ulibarri grant, swept clean of squatters, to a man who would discard it like a cigarette butt. He didn't care so much about the money; he could always make that; but the idea of Harvey Buckner, lord of these uncounted acres, reigning in his place was a hard thing to swallow. He couldn't let that happen. He would have to kill Buckner. But, outside of the satisfaction it would give him, what would he get out of it? Nothing.

But wait! If he could get Buckner's charter before killing him, maybe he could make a deal with Mary Buckner. With that charter, she could get the Ulibarri acres. But would she need it? Was there anybody besides himself, those squatters now vanished, and Mary Buckner herself who knew that Buckner was her uncle and not her father? With Buckner dead, couldn't she simply step in as the sole heir to her so-called father's estate and claim the Ulibarri grant without a charter? She could. Very well, then, he must fix it so that the true story would come out, that the Buckner in this room was her uncle, not her father. Once that was done, she would have need of the charter, for Harvey Buckner's will would dispose of the grant to charity. To get the grant, she must produce evidence that it belonged to her, not him. Very well, he must first get the charter. After that, he must break the story of the true relationship between Mary and Harvey Buckner. And then the way would be cleared for the sale of the charter to Mary Buckner.

He considered all this in silence, while Harvey Buckner regarded him with some curiosity.

"No more questions?" Buckner asked.

"No."

"Then get out. I'd like to sleep."

Still Bonsell thought. Finally he thought he had the plan. It would be risky, but it was worth trying. He was in a position of having to create a market for something he wanted to sell. Good.

He rose slowly, and the grin on his face was sheepish. "I've thought it all out," he told Buckner. "I'm licked. I haven't got a chance." He paused, smiling amiably now. "You know, I never thought you were that smart, Buckner."

"Most people don't," Buckner said modestly.

"You trimmed me in royal style."

"Didn't I?"

Bonsell scratched his head. "Funny, I ought to be sore as hell about it. I'm not."

"I wondered why you didn't blow up."

"It's so neat, I feel like a kid," Bonsell explained. "I thought I was a growed man. I'm not. I'm just a sucker, a pretty rosy one, too."

Buckner grinned. "Yes, pretty rosy."

"Well, I'll hit the trail. I just wanted you to know that it's the slickest thing I ever saw pulled, just from one crook to another."

Buckner laughed, and so did Bonsell.

"Thanks," Buckner said.

Bonsell slowly put out his hand. "Well, so long, Buckner. You're a better man than any I ever met."

Buckner smiled and put out his hand, too. Bonsell took it. "No hard feelings?" Buckner asked.

Bonsell yanked on Buckner's hand, drawing the arm tight, and then slugged him with his left fist, driving it hard into the temple. Buckner had no time to duck. The blow fell like a sledge, and he sprawled out on the bed, unconscious.

Bonsell worked carefully. He took a pillow, slipped off the pillowcase, drew his gun, placed the pillow on Buckner's chest, buried the muzzle of his gun in the pillow, and fired it. The sound was muffled, hardly audible.

He slapped out the fire that started in the pillow and then slipped the pillow back in the pillowcase. He wanted this to be a neat job.

Looking over at Buckner, he saw the man was dead. Arranging the pillow on the bed again, he came over to the door and listened. There was not a sound in the corridor.

The rest of his movements were leisurely. He searched

through Buckner's clothes until he found a pencil and a piece of paper. He wrote on the paper: *Meet me in the lobby at once if you want to find out about Harvey Buckner.*

That done, he turned the light dim, stepped out into the corridor, and walked down it to the corner room.

He tapped on the door and said softly, "Miss Buckner. Miss Buckner."

At the fourth try, a sleepy voice said, "Yes?"

"Gent downstairs left a note. I'll shove it under the door."

He did, and went swiftly back to Buckner's room. In five minutes he heard Mary Buckner pass on her way downstairs.

He slipped out in the corridor and into her room. The lamp was lighted. He picked a crumpled handkerchief from her dresser, then tore a strip of cloth out of a dressing-gown thrown over the foot of her bed.

Back in Buckner's room he listened until Mary came back upstairs. The clerk was with her, and he heard them talking in the corridor. Presently the clerk went downstairs.

Turning up the lamp, Bonsell arranged things the way he wanted them. He put the strip of cloth in Buckner's hand. He dropped the handkerchief under the chair. He took Buckner's gun, a Colt .45 with scarred cedar handles identical to his own, and exchanged them, placing the gun on the bed.

With one last look about him, he turned the lamp dim, opened the window, and drew his gun.

Pointing it at the sky, he fired once, then closed the window, dropped to the ground, and ran for his horse.

Slowly, then, he rode out of town, just as a lamp was lighted in one of the hotel rooms where the shot had been heard.

Chapter Fifteen: "HE'S BUSTED BANKS BEFORE."

MARY BUCKNER WAS NOT YET ASLEEP when she heard the shot. Like everyone else in the hotel, she was startled by it. Rising and throwing her wrapper about her, she wondered if the shot had any connection with that mysterious note she had just received. She was still angry over having had to dress and go down to the lobby, only to be told that she must have been dreaming, that nobody was waiting for her.

She peered out into the corridor, to find all the other doors open. A horse trader, galluses trailing down his legs, had pulled on his pants over his nightshirt and was standing in the middle of the hall, scratching his head when the clerk mounted the stairs.

Several others trailed out of their rooms, asking, "What happened?"

The horse trader answered them all with a "Damfino," and said to the clerk, "A shot woke us up."

"Was it here in the building?"

"Sure sounded like it. On that side of the building."

The clerk looked at the doors. They were all open, with persons standing in them, except one, and that was the door to Buckner's room. Mary came out and joined the others, her curiosity whetted.

The horse trader noticed the closed door and went over and knocked on it. There was no answer, and he asked the clerk, "Who's in there?"

"I'll have to look at the register."

"Hell, I don't aim to call him by his name," the horse trader growled. He pounded on the door. "Hey, open up if you're there!" Still no answer.

"Try the door," the clerk suggested.

The horse trader opened it, and the others crowded toward it. There lay Buckner dead on the bed. At sight of him the horse trader whistled and entered the room. The others shoved in behind him. Mary, since nobody had spoken a word, came up to the door last. The watchers were so scattered that she could see Buckner's form lying on the bed.

The sight of him made her gasp, attracting the horse trader's attention. He turned to Buckner, lifted the strip of cloth from his hand and looked at Mary. "Well, well," he said slowly.

He came across the room, put the cloth against Mary's dressing-gown, and said nothing, only looked at her.

It took Mary a full second to understand what he was doing, and then the color flushed out of her face.

"Do you know this man?" the horse trader asked curiously, pointing to Buckner.

"Y—Yes."

That was all there was to it. The clerk got the sheriff. The sheriff got Cope. When they got there, Mary was crying on the chair under which the horse trader had already found the handkerchief. A sheet was thrown over Buckner.

Cope stormed in, his face dark with fury, and Mary rushed to his arms. His first words were matter-of-fact ones. He told her to go dress. His next were addressed to the morbid watchers, and he told them to get the hell out of there.

His next move was to go over and look at Buckner.

"How'd you find him?" he asked the horse trader. He was told. Immediately he went down to Mary's room and came back with the dressing-gown. It was Sheriff Link Haynes who found where the piece was torn out.

Cope said, "I don't believe it."

"You got eyes, ain't you?" the horse trader said.

"Mister," Cope said in a voice filled with quiet menace,

"I raised that girl."

"Looks like you done a damn poor job of it," the horse trader opined.

Cope was on him in a second. It took Sheriff Haynes and two others to get Cope off, and the horse trader slunk out of the room, nursing a bloody nose.

When the sheriff, Cope, and the clerk were alone again, Cope said to Haynes, "Well, what are you goin' to do?"

Haynes said quietly, "That's her father, isn't it?"

Cope nodded.

"And they've fought?"

"Who said so?"

"She told Kling the other day that she didn't know or care about her father. She was huffy."

"What does that prove?" Cope snarled.

"Take it easy," Haynes said. "It proves they weren't friendly."

"Does it prove she killed him?"

"She was awake five minutes before. She came down to the clerk with a cock-and-bull story. She didn't like her father. A piece of her clothes was found in his hand. Her handkerchief was found under the chair. What am I supposed to believe, if I won't believe my eyes?"

"I tell you she didn't do it!" Cope said angrily.

"Then who did?"

"I don't know. But she didn't!"

Haynes looked at Cope a long time. "All right, Cope, that's what you say. But I've talked to men who saw Buckner in Sante Fe years back. He told them that he thought his daughter was crazy, and that sometimes he was afraid of her. If all those things don't add to one thing, then I can't count."

"But she's a girl!"

"A girl can shoot a gun, can't she?"

Cope was wordless. What was there to say, except to

blindly reiterate his belief that Mary Buckner was innocent?

Haynes listened and didn't comment until Cope was through. Then he said, "I don't know why she shot him, Cope. Maybe he got rough. Maybe he threatened her. Maybe she shot him in self-defense. I dunno why she did, but it looks like she shot him. And I got to arrest her."

"Jail her?"

Cope exploded again at Haynes's nod, but Mary's entrance cut him short. Then Haynes began to question her. He was finished by daylight, and not once during those hours did she change her story. No, she didn't like her father. Yes, she knew he was here. No, she hadn't talked to him. No, she didn't kill him. No, she didn't know how the cloth got in his hands. She showed Haynes the note that was stuck under her door in the night. Haynes looked skeptical. If it was true, then it was only Buckner's ruse to get her out of bed to come to his room. And she shot him; there was no doubt about it.

The upshot was that Mary had breakfast in the hotel dining-room and afterward was taken to the new jail. Cope was furious, but Link Haynes was as stubborn as a weak man could be. The Excelsior outfit, the Buckners and Bonsell, the squatters and their rights—all of these he was heartily sick of. Reports had been sifting through to him of fights between Bonsell and the squatters. He couldn't find the truth anywhere. Everybody was lying. When he accosted Cruver on the street and asked him about the reports, Cruver told him to mind his own damn business. There was nothing a man could go against, only rumors.

But he could get his teeth into this. And like all indecisive men, when he made up his mind, he had made it up for good. Mary Buckner hadn't ever asked his help. He didn't know why she was here, only he supposed it was something to do with the Excelsior, some trouble she was going to straighten out with her father. Well, she had gone too far.

Mary went docilely into the cell while Cope stirred up the town with his wrath. Strangely enough, he found it divided in sentiment. There were many who never liked Buckner, and who remembered that story Mary Buckner had tried to spread about her father's death. They didn't like her either. They didn't like the Buckners' uppish ways. They thought Haynes was justified in holding her.

At eight o'clock, the mail was distributed, and Link Haynes, sick of Cope's rowing, walked over alone to get his mail at the post office. He came back considerably faster than he went, and entered the new cell block without any ceremony. He would not let Cope come in with him.

"Miss Buckner," he began, "I got a letter in the mail this mornin' about you."

"What about me?"

Haynes looked wise. "James Buckner wasn't your father. He wasn't James Buckner. He was your uncle Harvey, posin' as your father. That was the cause of the fight. That's why you murdered him."

Mary Buckner's wan face, for the first time, wore a look of uneasiness, and Link Haynes knew that the writer of this anonymous letter had been right.

In the absence of Cope, he started a gentle bullying, but he soon abandoned it. He didn't need it. Mary had given herself away. The look of guilt on her face was interpreted by Haynes as a confession. To right that impression, Mary told him that James Buckner was Harvey Buckner, and that the letter had been correct. That only strengthened Haynes's belief that she had committed the murder. He hated to think as pretty a girl as this would murder her father. An uncle made it easier. It also made a neater case for him. She wouldn't tell him how it happened that Harvey Buckner owned the Ulibarri acres, while she was left

penniless by her father, but he surmised that James Buckner had disinherited his daughter. That gave a motive for
the killing. He wanted to know about James Buckner, too,
but again Mary would tell him nothing. The only confession that ever passed her lips was the fact that the Buckner
who had been killed was her uncle.

Haynes came away from that session a little puzzled, but
confident that he was on the right track. As for holding a
woman, wasn't she a murderer? Maybe a jury wouldn't
convict her, but he would have done his duty in bringing
her to trial.

When he stepped out into the office, Cope was still there,
huge and sweating and angry as a bull. His crutch kept
tap-tapping on the floor in impatience.

"You still here?" Haynes growled.

"I want to know things," Cope said. "Where is the man
who rode in here with Buckner yesterday?"

"Who was that?"

"How the hell would I know? That's your job. He
brought a man with him from Sante Fe. A lantern-jawed
gunnie that looked like he'd kill a man for the price of a
drink. Go find him!"

"All right."

"Another thing. Have you had Bonsell in here? He's another killer. He was partners with Buckner in the Excelsior. How do you know he didn't kill Buckner over the
ranch?"

"I don't."

"Then find out!" Cope raved. "You've grabbed an innocent girl on a simple frame-up, Link, and damned if I'm
goin' to let you stop there! Get those two to start with! And
another thing. Who sent that letter to you this mornin'?"

"What letter?" Haynes asked blankly.

"Why, you damn fool, I heard you bullyin' her into ad-
mitting that Buckner was her uncle. Who sent the letter?"

"I don't know."

"Find out! Find out!" Cope raved. "Get out of here and do something!"

Sheriff Link Haynes was simply overwhelmed by Cope's fury. Fortunately for him, Max Bonsell and a stranger rode into town at nine o'clock and pulled up at the Exchange House tie rail. Bonsell had picked Ray Warren up on the road. Warren's horse had thrown a shoe last night and had gone lame. Early this morning, on his way to town, Max Bonsell had ridden into his camp. Seeing his plight, he had gone back to the hide-out for another horse and they had ridden in together.

Link Haynes saw them and went over to them as they dismounted.

"Where you two goin'?" he asked bluntly.

Bonsell regarded him coldly. "Well, it ain't much of your business, Haynes, but we're goin' in the hotel to see a man."

"Who?"

Bonsell looked at Warren and then back at Haynes. "Why, man by the name of Buckner."

"He's dead," Haynes announced bluntly. "Murdered last night."

Bonsell and Warren only stared at him, and then Warren said, "Jim Buckner murdered? Here?"

Haynes nodded. "Where were you two last night?"

Bonsell said quickly, "At my camp."

"Both of you?"

"Yes."

"Any proof?"

"All you want," Bonsell drawled, and then asked, "How'd he die?"

"Never mind that," Haynes said. "I want to talk to you two. Come over to the office."

At the office, Haynes ordered Cope out and then began

his examination of the two men. Both were closemouthed about their business with Buckner, saying only that their business was none of Haynes's. Warren crawled under the shelter of Max Bonsell's lie with a certain thankfulness, since a night spent alone at the time of a murder would place him as a suspect. Bonsell knew this, and he swore innocently that he and Warren had been at his camp with some men, some men he hired as a skeleton crew to man the Excelsior.

Haynes got nowhere. When he was finished, Bonsell spoke his mind. He said he thought it was a particularly offensive act on Haynes's part to arrest Mary Buckner as a suspect. In a roundabout way, and with a perfectly expressionless face, he said insulting things about Haynes's intelligence until the sheriff's face was red as brick. Bonsell finished, "Since you've got her in jail here, I don't suppose anybody can talk to her but you."

"I didn't say that!"

"Then I'd like to speak to her," Bonsell said. "If what you say is true that Jim Buckner was her uncle and not her father, that still makes her take over the Ulibarri grant, don't it? And if it does, she's my boss. And I'd like to talk to her and get some orders."

Haynes took Bonsell's gun and let him into the cell block. Mary was seated on a bench, her head bowed, but when she heard the door open, she looked up.

Her brown eyes plainly told Bonsell that he was not welcome. For his part, he was a perfect gentleman. He drawled a good morning, took his hat off, and bluntly announced that he thought Haynes was a fool for doing this to her. Haynes slammed the door, and they were alone.

Mary looked at Bonsell with some curiosity in her glance. This was the man that had framed Jim Ward so neatly, a merciless gunman from Texas, Jim had said. He certainly didn't look the part, but Mary was not fooled.

She said coldly, "I don't imagine we have much to talk about, have we? Under what pretense did you get in here, anyway?"

"I'm still the ramrod for Excelsior, Miss Buckner," Bonsell said humbly. "My boss is dead. You're his daughter so you're my boss."

"I wish I were," Mary said bitterly, her brown eyes flashing. "Let's drop the pretense. Both you and I know that James Buckner over there in the hotel wasn't my father. So does Haynes. What do you want?"

"Does the Ulibarri grant go to you now, Miss Buckner?" Bonsell asked.

"You know it doesn't!" Mary flared. "You've taken enough pains in these last years to make sure I never get it!" She paused, eying his cool, bland features with their smoky, expressionless eyes. "I've often thought that you're probably the man who stole the charter out of my trunk up in Wyoming."

Bonsell colored a little at that. "You haven't accused me yet of killin' Buckner."

"You probably did!" she said swiftly.

Max Bonsell grinned amiably. "Now, I've never torn up that kind of a meal ticket in my life, Miss Buckner. Give me credit for some sense."

"Then what do you want with me?"

"I only wondered what yuh aimed to do when you get out of here. I mean, are you goin' to take to the law courts over the grant?"

"Of course."

"Goin' to try and prove that Buckner was your uncle, not your father?"

"I am."

"How?"

"By proving he was a fraud."

"I know, but how?"

"There must be some way," Mary said coldly. "He's made a slip somewhere."

Bonsell conceded that. "But to prove he's your uncle, you got to prove your father's dead. And even you have got to admit that can't be done. You can't even find his grave."

Mary said, "And how do you know all this? How do you know what I'll have to do in court?" Her intuition prompted the next remark. "Did he make you his heir, by any chance?"

Bonsell smiled and held up his hands. "He did not," he said grinning. "That would make too nice a case for murder against me. No, he didn't leave me a thing—except the disposal of some of his papers."

Mary missed that last remark, but Bonsell was patient.

"Then what do you want? What are you trying to tell me? That I have a long fight ahead of me to prove my identity, and that I have a slim chance of taking over my property?"

"That's about it," Bonsell said.

"How does that concern you?"

"Well, what if I made it easier for you?"

"You mean testify that James Buckner was Harvey Buckner?"

Bonsell laughed. "No such thing. I'll never be dragged into a court, Miss Buckner."

"Then how?"

"Isn't there something else that would help you?"

"Nothing short of—" She paused and looked keenly at him. "You mean the charter?"

Bonsell nodded.

Mary had her mouth open to say, "But it's in the bank under his name and nobody can touch it except his heirs," but something warned her to keep silent. She said in a small voice, "Oh."

"Wouldn't that help you?"

Mary nodded. "Have you got it?"

This time Bonsell nodded.

"How did you get it?"

Bonsell rolled a smoke and lighted it. "I'm goin' to tell you somethin', Miss Buckner, about me and your uncle. We aren't what you'd call trustful men. We've both had to live by our wits, and the law could take us for a lot of things if it could prove its case. Now, when we threw in together to do you out of the Ulibarri grant, it was risky." He smiled suddenly. "I'm talkin' pretty blunt."

"No blunter than I want. It's not news to me."

"All right. When we made our plans, we saw it was risky. Also, there was no assurance that we wouldn't double-cross each other if we got a chance."

"I can understand that," Mary said dryly.

"On the other hand, if we were square with each other, we both stood to profit. But Buckner wanted to make sure of one thing. That was, that I wouldn't kill him if I saw a chance to grab the Ulibarri grant by myself."

"You're both lovely men, I know," Mary commented.

Bonsell ignored her. "So he couldn't make me his heir. He figured I'd kill him if he did. But in case of his accidental death, he wanted to leave me somethin'. Can't you guess what it was?"

"The charter?"

"That's it. He left me the charter. And whoever was goin' to take over the Ulibarri grant—his heirs, you, your folks, or a shyster outfit would have to have the charter. That left me with the charter to bargain with. That was my reward for shootin' square with him." He paused. "Well, I got the charter. What's it worth to you?"

"You mean you're trying to sell it to me so I can prove title to the Ulibarri grant?"

"That's it to a hair. What's it worth to you?"

"But I haven't any money."

"If you get the charter you will have. In the neighborhood of half a million dollars, maybe more."

"But I can't get your charter without money."

"I'll trust you."

"You'll what?" Mary asked, amazement in her voice.

"I'll trust you," Bonsell said placidly. "Look here, Miss Buckner. I may have done a lot of things in my life that wouldn't stand a too close look. But I've learned to judge people. I know an honest person, a fine woman when I see one. You're both. Your note would be as good as gold with me, even if I couldn't go to a court to collect it. That'd be enough, just your note." Bonsell, for once, was telling the truth. He never doubted Mary's honesty. All a man had to do was look at her to know that. She was a person who would keep her word to a dog. And that one point was what Bonsell counted on. In a year, he would have that money from her, with only her promise as security. Even if he was proven ten times over a murderer, Mary Buckner would keep her promise. And, far from considering his attitude strange, Bonsell thought it only natural.

Mary looked at Bonsell a long moment. "That's quite a compliment, considering the source of it."

Bonsell only grinned. "You'll admit you need it."

"Yes."

"Then it's yours for fifty thousand dollars."

Mary said, "Isn't that quite a bit?"

"Less than ten percent of what the Ulibarri grant is worth." He rose. "Think it over, Miss Buckner. I'll be back tomorrow."

He left then. Mary called Sheriff Haynes and asked if she could see Cope.

When Cope came, she told him of Bonsell's offer. Cope left and went over to his rooms. Jim Wade was pacing the floor, his gray eyes hot with an anger that was almost choking him.

He whirled at Cope's entrance and said, "Have they let her out?"

Cope shook his head and pushed Jim down into a chair. 'Listen to this," he said, and told him of Bonsell's offer.

For a long moment, Jim said nothing, staring at Cope. Then he said, "But the charter's in the bank!"

"That's what we thought."

"But it is!" Jim insisted vehemently. "We know Buckner brought the charter with him because he told Scoville so. Would he keep it in his room?"

"It don't look like it."

"Would he keep it on him?"

"No."

"Then where else could it be if it isn't in the bank?"

"But how can Bonsell get it if it's in the bank?" Cope said gloomily. "The bank won't give it to him. No, it's got to be somewhere else."

Jim sat motionless for a moment, then comprehension flooded his face. He bounded up and grabbed Cope by the arm.

"We're fools, Cope, fools! Of course it's in the bank! Don't you see? Bonsell's goin' to bust the bank open and take it!"

Cope scowled, watching him.

"I know Bonsell," Jim said, more quietly. "He never thinks of the risk in anything. What he wants, he'll take. He's busted banks before. He'll bust this one. He'll take all the cash he can find and rifle the boxes in the vault. And you'll find when he's done, the charter is gone out of Buckner's box. It'll pop up next week or so and cost Mary fifty thousand dollars."

Cope said, "But he'd give himself away."

"Who to?" Jim countered. "Nobody knows what's in that box but us and Warren. Warren, he can take care of. But he doesn't know we know it. Even the bank doesn't know it. That makes it easy, doesn't it?"

He started pacing the floor again, and Cope watched him, letting this piece of information turn over in his mind. It sounded logical. It sounded like Max Bonsell.

Jim paused and said quietly, "Also, he's the coyote that nailed Buckner."

"Why do you think that?"

"Easy," Jim said grimly. "Scoville convinced Buckner that Bonsell was double-crossing him. They had a row, and Buckner kicked Bonsell out. Bonsell just had a fortune taken away from him. What's left to be done? Get even with Buckner. But there was no information he could peddle to Mary that she didn't know already. There was only one way to make money from his knowledge. That was to get the charter and sell it to Mary. So he got even with Buckner by killing him. And he'll make his money on the charter. That could happen, couldn't it?"

"It could," Cope conceded.

"It did," Jim said. He paused at one of the heavily curtained windows and looked over the roofs of the town. He felt like a trapped animal, helpless. As long as daylight lasted, he was penned up in these rooms, and could only try to walk his restlessness off. In the jail across the street, they were holding Mary Buckner, an innocent girl, on the rottenest frame-up charge possible. He had to throttle the impulse to tuck a gun in his waist, go out in broad daylight, and kill the man who tried to stop him from taking Mary Buckner out of that jail. But it wouldn't help—except to prove to the world that Mary Buckner was guilty.

He wheeled to face Cope. "What time is the preliminary hearing set for?"

"Eleven o'clock. In ten minutes."

"Got the bail?"

"Five thousand, right in my pocket."

Jim swore darkly and resumed his pacing. Cope left, and

the place was silent. Ben Beauchamp was in Cope's bed sleeping. Jim tried to quiet his racing brain by guessing at Bonsell's plans. If Bonsell robbed the bank, it would be at night. Tonight? Maybe, maybe not. He'd be there to see, anyway.

Even the thought of Bonsell brought red murder to his mind. Why not slip out tonight, wait for Bonsell or hunt him down and kill him? No, his judgment told him that was poor planning. Bonsell must be caught with the goods, and the capture must prove that Mary was innocent of Buckner's murder, must prove her title to the grant, and prove his own innocence. But how could it all be done? He didn't know.

He paced the floor, clenching his fists till his knuckles were white. His pipe tasted foul, and he put it away without smoking. And he sat there, boiling—and helpless.

Chapter Sixteen: OLD ENEMIES—NEW PARTNERS

BONSELL WAS UNDECIDED about two or three things, but they would work themselves out. After he left Mary, he arranged for Buckner's burial which would be in the afternoon. After the arrangements, he and Warren left the hardware store, in the back of which were the undertaking parlors.

On the street, Warren said, "I'm much obliged for givin' me an alibi for last night."

Bonsell murmured, *"Por nada*—for nothing. No use givin' Haynes a chance to rawhide you when I could keep him from it, was there?"

Warren said no. He rolled a smoke and lighted it and then observed, "The funny part of it is, I had the chance to murder him and you had the motive to." He looked at Bonsell. "We weren't together last night. Neither one of us knows whether the other one did it."

"What motive would I have had?" Bonsell asked.

"You double-crossed him on that false corner, didn't you? When he saw you, he would have fired you."

"So that's what he was goin' to see me about?" Bonsell murmured. "Well, well. How'd he spot that?"

"Scoville took him to see it."

"Scoville's dead."

"Prob'ly wasn't his name."

Bonsell smiled. "No, and I can tell you his name. It was Jim Wade. Remember me writin' the boss about the way I hung that squatter trouble on Wade?"

"Yeah, I got the letter here."

"Read it careful, then. I told you he broke jail and disappeared. Last week one of my riders spotted that false corner, and a man workin' on it. It was Wade, and he drove Wade off." Bonsell laughed. "Did Wade send for Buckner?"

"Wrote him a letter."

"And Buckner talked to him before he talked to me?"

Warren nodded, watching Bonsell carefully. Bonsell only shook his head and said in a tone of injury, "Now why didn't he come to me right off? Pardee could have told him the whole story."

"You knew it, then?"

"Knew it! It's in the letter that's waitin' for Buckner in Sante Fe now," Bonsell lied. "Could I tell him about it any faster? I wrote as soon as I went over and saw it for myself."

Warren was silent a long moment, teetering on the edge of the boardwalk. "That's mighty queer," he said, at last.

"What is?"

"Why, yesterday, I'd of sworn you was guilty of tryin' to double-cross Buckner. I reckon I acted sort of short last night."

"I didn't notice it if you did," Bonsell said blandly.

"Well, and now you tell me this mornin' what it's all about. And it sounds so damn simple, I'm wondering why both me and Buckner got up on our hind legs."

Bonsell nodded thoughtfully. "If he'd only talked to me first. He ought to know I'd never try and get away with a thing like that, even if he didn't trust me. Wade, I reckon, hoped he'd do just that. Wade was trying to break our partnership."

"I can see that now."

"Too bad Buckner couldn't."

Warren dropped his cigarette. "Who killed Buckner, Bonsell?"

Bonsell scowled thoughtfully. "I dunno. What happened out there at the corner?"

Warren told him. When he was finished Bonsell snapped his fingers. "Then you never saw Wade go back to town?"

"No."

"How do you know he wasn't followin' you?"

"Maybe he was."

"And when he saw Buckner ride into town instead of high-tailin' it to me, he thought Buckner wasn't goin' to do anything about it. He saw where his plan didn't work. But he still aimed to square things with the Excelsior. So he sneaked up to Buckner's room, knowin' you'd be gone, because he'd seen you go."

"But what about draggin' that girl into it?"

"She's a Buckner, ain't she? He don't know anything about the girl's fight with Buckner."

Warren thought this over a moment, then said, "So it's Wade?"

"Who else could it be?"

"Well, I'm damned," Warren said.

Bonsell left him that way, saying he'd meet him around town. Walking over to the bank, he smiled to himself at Warren's gullibility. Maybe he could use the man.

At the bank, Bonsell asked for Charles Mitchell, the president. He wanted to straighten out Buckner's affairs, he said, and close the Excelsior account. It took a little time, and all the time he was there he was examining the bank, its locks, its windows, its bars, its vault. Nothing escaped him, for his was a practiced eye. He saw the single rack of safety boxes against the left wall. They were steel boxes, labeled and locked. He didn't inquire if Buckner had a safety-deposit box, because it was too risky. He simply gave the name of the Sante Fe bank where Buckner's will was, and left.

He ate at the Exchange House dining-room at a table by himself. The talk was all of Buckner's murder, but he gave no opinions.

After dinner, he loafed around the plaza. Soon he saw Will-John Cruver go into the Freighter's Pleasure. He followed him and saw him standing at the bar. There were only a few men in the saloon, and those were either playing in the game of poker or watching it. Cope wasn't around.

Bonsell called for a whisky and saw in the bar mirror that Cruver was regarding him without any fear at all. The bartender brought the bottle and glass to Bonsell, then retired to his newspaper at the end of the bar. If he was surprised at seeing the heads of two warring factions drinking quietly at the same bar, he did not show it.

Presently, Bonsell turned his head and said quietly, "Haven't seen you around much, Will-John. Where you been?"

"Buryin' people," Cruver answered.

Bonsell smiled a little and said, "Now that the war's over, we can buy each other a drink, can't we?"

Cruver said, "Who said it was over?"

"You aimin' to carry it on by yourself?"

"Don't know but what I will," Cruver said.

Bonsell slapped a half dollar on the counter and said softly, "We might talk it over downstreet."

He paid up and went out. Cruver followed him after a half minute's interval. Bonsell headed for the Mexican cantina off the plaza. It was a low adobe affair of a single room that was cool in the midday sun.

He was sitting at a table when Cruver walked in and took a chair opposite him. Bonsell called in Spanish for a bottle of whisky and two glasses, and then poured the drinks.

"Well, it looks sort of tough for us both," Bonsell announced.

"You out of your job?"

Bonsell nodded. "The Buckner girl will take over in a little while and she can't use me. You, either."

"I don't know about that," Cruver drawled.

"Make no mistake," Bonsell went on. "She's the rightful heir. All the fightin' done around here will be you against the U.S. marshal."

Cruver shrugged.

"I hate to leave the place without takin' a little somethin' with me," Bonsell murmured.

Cruver's crafty eyes narrowed. "Like what?"

"Money."

"Where'll you get it?"

"Where most people put it."

"The bank, hunh?"

Bonsell shrugged. "Ever bust a bank? Know anything about it?"

Cruver shook his head.

"This one's easy," Bonsell said. "I happen to know that Buckner deposited twenty thousand in it the day he got here."

Cruver's eyes lighted up.

"But you ain't interested," Bonsell went on. "You're

goin' to stick here and fight, you said."

"Not if I can get out with money."

Bonsell smiled suddenly. "You can. I need another man."

It didn't seem peculiar to either of them that they should throw together. After all, Bonsell's status was that of a paid fighting man, and Cruver had been illegally holding land that did not belong to him. Underneath they were of the same stripe, Bonsell with the brains, the quickness, Cruver with the strength and the stubbornness. It occurred to both of them that they were admirable partners, and that they were wasting their time fighting each other. Bonsell named the meeting-place and left. Cruver stayed long enough to finish the bottle of whisky, reflecting on his great good fortune.

Buckner's funeral was a hurried affair. A hired buckboard was the hearse, and Germany Kling, a pious sort of man, offered to officiate. Link Haynes, Kling, Bonsell, and Warren were the only ones attending. It was significant that Harvey Buckner, who had been friendless in life, had only a hired preacher, a suspicious lawman, and two hired gunmen to put him to rest.

Afterward, Kling and Haynes rode home in the buckboard, and Warren and Bonsell went to their horses. The Spanish gravedigger was already at his work.

"What do you aim to do now?" Bonsell asked Warren.

"Ride."

"Want to bust a bank before we leave?" Bonsell asked casually. There was no use mincing words; Warren was a man like himself.

Warren regarded him soberly. "Is it worth it?"

"I dunno. Cope coins money in that place of his. He uses this bank. That alone ought to be worth it."

Warren agreed, much as he would have agreed to a drink in the nearest saloon.

"Then get your war bag. Stop in at Haynes's office, tell him you're ridin', then hit the trail. Tonight we'll meet." He named the place. At the plaza, they shook hands in public and parted, and Warren went on to the sheriff's office.

Bonsell watched him go, a wicked smile on his face. Two fools, Warren and Cruver.

Chapter Seventeen: "COME AND GET ME!"

As SOON AS DARK CAME, Jim, Scoville, and Ben slipped out to the edge of town where they got the horses Scoville had left there. Once mounted, they sought the alleys and without any difficulty achieved the one that ran past the rear of the bank. Scoville then took the horses, went up the alley with them, and tied them at the hitchrail that ran alongside the sheriff's office.

When he came back, Jim had chosen their hiding-places. One was in the shed directly back of the bank. That was Scoville's and Ben's place. His own was immediately behind the board fence adjoining the shed.

Jim judged that while Bonsell would have preferred many hours of darkness in which to get away after the robbery, he could not risk an attempt early in the evening. The robbery would take place after the town had emptied, and while it was asleep. Nevertheless, Jim could not take the risk of missing him.

They squatted inside the shed to wait, and the hours dragged by. None of them said much, Jim Wade least of all. He had known anger before, but the sight of Mary Buckner when she came to Cope's rooms, smiling but lost and afraid, had done something to him. He felt like a machine now, intent on only one thing—to punish Bonsell for hurting her. It was a different kind of anger, a cool one, a killing one, the kind a man experienced when he saw a man reach for a gun and knew that he himself must reach faster and shoot straighter. A man couldn't afford a hot anger then, and Jim Wade couldn't now.

Toward midnight the noises of the town ceased. That meant the stores were closing, and that people had sought their homes.

But it was closer to one o'clock when Ben, on watch, whispered, "Here comes a bunch of riders."

Jim went to the door and counted them, then motioned Ben back to latch the door from the inside. He himself slipped behind the fence, and waited until they approached. There were three of them, and they were not talking.

He heard them stop not twenty feet from him, and a man's voice, Bonsell's, said finally, "Well, here she is, gents."

"Back door and window have got bars over 'em, ain't they?" a strange voice asked.

"Unh-hunh. So's the front." That was Cruver's voice. Cruver and Bonsell together! That didn't make sense. On second thought, it did, too, for they were alike in many ways, apt to pool their resources once they quit fighting each other.

"Don't worry about that," Bonsell said quietly. "There's a roof on the place, ain't there?"

"That what you brought the crowbar for?" Cruver asked.

"You watch. Here. Take these tow-sacks and the dynamite. And, for God's sake, be careful of it."

They dismounted, leading their horses close behind the bank and tethering them at the bars of the window.

There was a lot of quiet business that Jim could hear but not see. The proximity of their horses to the rear door meant that they were not going to blow through the rear entrance, at least.

And then Jim saw them on the roof. So Bonsell had spotted the skylights as the weakest place! But once they achieved the ridge of the bank's roof, they went no farther.

Cruver said querulously, "What you goin' to do, Bonsell? Cut a hole in the damn thing?"

"You wait," Bonsell said. The first thing he did was rip away the tar paper on the roof. There were three layers of it, and he peeled it off quickly. Then he said, "Yeah, just what I thought. The roof is like any other buildin'." He turned to Cruver. "Why try to tear an iron bar out when all you got to do is pry off a board?"

He proceeded to do so. The boards ran from the ridge to the eaves. He pried off five of them. Then he came to the subroofing, which was laid diagonally. He got the ends of three of those boards loose, propped them up, slipped in between the rafters, and disappeared inside. There was some talk between them that Jim couldn't hear, but it was probably Bonsell telling them that there was a ceiling over the room and to hand the crowbar down.

At any rate, Cruver handed it to him. Jim heard a couple of muffled blows, which would be sufficient to break the lath over the ceiling. Then Cruver and the stranger slipped through the roof and disappeared.

Jim came out to join Scoville and Ben.

"Well, I'm damned," Scoville murmured. "Just took the roof off, hunh?"

Inside Bonsell lowered himself to a desk from one of the rafters and took the dynamite from Cruver, who then came down. Warren was last.

Bonsell told them his plan. "Whatever jughead—a bunch of Mexs, I suppose—done the stonework on that vault, he left a couple of small holes for ventilation. That's where the dynamite goes. You two jaspers go up in front and lie down on the floor. After she blows, Warren, you stay there at the front door and watch. Whoever tries to get in, knock out that glass and cut down on him. Will-John, you take the back door. There's two locks. A hasp on the bars comes through the wooden door to padlock to a staple inside. Shoot it off first. Then there's the lock on the wood door. Shoot that off, unbolt the bolts, and we're away. You do that while I'm gettin' the loot. Now you got it?"

They said they had. After they had moved two desks together so they afforded adequate shelter against the blast, Bonsell went up to the vault.

Toward the top there was a small, square hole, big enough for three sticks of dynamite. Bonsell didn't need that many but he wanted to make sure. He uncoiled the fuse, slipped the caps on, and then tucked the dynamite in the hole.

He saw no sense in a long wait, so he cut the fuse short, saw that all was ready, and called, "Lie down!"

Then he whipped a match across his pants, touched it to the fuse end, and ran.

He barely made the protection of the desk before the sharp, vicious explosion hammered out, seeming to suck all the air in the room to it. The floor seemed to lift and slide, there was a heavy muffled clap and then every window in the place shattered as something heavy collapsed.

Bonsell, a full wastebasket in his hand, was on his feet immediately, Cruver behind him. They parted at the vault, and Bonsell saw that a whole section of the stone vault lay open toward the top. He lifted his leg, placed it against the stone, and shoved. Four feet of the wall caved inside.

Once through the opening, he worked swiftly, without nervousness. He touched a match to the paper in the wastebasket, so that it served as a lamp. By its light, he read the names on the safe-deposit boxes until he came to Buckner's. He pulled out the box, shot the lock off, opened it, and saw the slim bundle of papers in the bottom. One was thick and wrapped in oilcloth, and he smiled at sight of it. He put all in his inside coat pocket.

Then he pulled out two or three other boxes, shot the locks off, and dumped their contents in the tow-sacks without looking at them. This would make the robbery of Buckner's box less noticeable.

Cruver's shooting was loud in that small room. He shot three times, swearing loudly. Bonsell moved up to the big cash box, opened it, dumped the contents in a sack, smiling at its meagerness, then proceeded to sweep papers, anything in sight, into the sack, also.

The light had gone out now, and Bonsell carefully set the sack down and moved to the opening. Through it, he could see Warren outlined against the dim lights of the town.

Drawing his gun, he rested it on a rock jutting from the jagged wall, took careful sight, and pulled the trigger. Warren went down without a sound.

He shuttled his gaze to Cruver. Cruver had stopped work, and was looking up at Warren. Again Bonsell raised his gun and fired. Cruver staggered back against the wall, tripped, fell, and rolled on his face. But he had his gun out and was fighting to get a sight at Bonsell.

Bonsell moved quick as a snake. He lunged for a desk, just as Cruver shot, and the slug ripped into the wood. With one great heave, he turned the desk over on Cruver, crushing his gun hand to the floor. He had shot Cruver in the chest. Why take time to kill him?

The sack of loot he left in the vault. Running up to Warren, he grabbed him by the back of his coat and hauled him back beside Cruver, then yanked Warren's gun out and shot it once. Cruver's boots kept tapping the floor as he kicked weakly. It would look now as if Cruver and Warren had got to fighting after the robbery and had killed each other.

He looked toward the front and heard men across the plaza yelling at each other. It was time to move. He went to the back door, yanked the wooden door open, and a blast of gunfire poured into it from Ben and Scoville. He slammed it quickly, looking up front again. Two men were running across the plaza. It looked as though they had him trapped, but Bonsell coolly surveyed his chances. There was always the roof.

He leaped to the desk, paused, caught his wind, then jumped for the rafter showing through the hole in the ceiling. He caught it and swung himself up and was soon on the roof. As he emerged, a shot from below whipped into a board beside his head.

He sent a snap shot at the flame, then started out across the roofs, crouching low, toward the livery stable.

Another shot reached out for him, the slug whipping into the roof. He turned in time to see a man's head vanish below a roof ridge. This man had taken to the roofs, too. Footsteps were pounding in the alley and he heard a man yell, "Get him on the street, Ben! He's got to come down!"

Bonsell was two roofs from the corner. He ran as hard as he could down the roof slope, jumped the gap, ran up the next, down it, and was on the wooden awning next the street. It was low; he did not even pause in his pace. He soared off the awning, lit in the street, rolled over with his momentum, gained his feet, all in one motion and streaked for the dark sanctuary of the feed-stable door. Shots kicked up dust around him as he raced, and one whipped into the archway frame a foot from his head as he sprawled onto the planking in the darkness.

And then Jim Wade came boiling over the roofs, just as Scoville and Ben came out of the alley. He jumped, just as Bonsell jumped, only did not fall.

Ben was streaking for the passageway between the stable nd saddle shop next door; Scoville cut across, without any rders, and rounded the corner on his way to the alley.

And Jim plunged into the darkness of the archway after Bonsell. Halfway down it, he heard two shots and saw a gun flash from the corral. Almost immediately there was another shot from the alley, and again, more to the left his time, the gun flash appeared.

And then Jim Wade smiled. Bonsell was trapped in the orral.

He slipped out the back door and flattened himself against the barn. Ben, at the far corner of the corral, laced a tentative shot into the darkness. It was answered immediately by Bonsell, who was standing almost in the middle f the corral. Scoville, in the alley at the other corner of he corral, took up firing on the heels of Bonsell's shooting.

And then there was a long silence in which horses norted and stamped.

"Bonsell!" Wade called.

There was a silence and then softly, "Who is it?"

"Jim Wade. Better give up."

"Be damned to you, Wade!" Bonsell snarled. "Come nd get me!"

"I'm comin'," Jim said quietly.

With a gun in each hand, he started to move slowly toward the middle of the corral, listening carefully for any novement other than that of the horses. Bonsell shot at im once, but it was wide of the mark, and Jim answered. Bonsell laughed softly, his voice seeming to come out of a dozen places in the night.

The darkness was a great void which, to a man's eyes, ouched infinity. Sifting through it came the shouting of he men at the bank and the small noises of an awakening own. But here it was silent, with a thin, wire-taut tension to it that screwed a man's nerves tight and wild.

And then, at Scoville's end of the corral, a light appeared over the sheds and began to grow.

Bonsell laid five shots in the direction of the fire, panic seizing him. Still, only the blurred dark forms of the horses were visible.

Suddenly, like a meteor in the sky, a flaming barrel lifted over the corral poles and crashed into the corral lot. It was a trash barrel holding paper. Scoville had dragged it up behind a shed, lighted the paper and allowed it to catch, covered with boards to hide the flames, and then had tossed it over the poles.

When it landed, it spilled out a smear of burning paper, pushing the night back beyond the corral poles.

There was a stirring among the horses, and then Bonsell, in his sock feet, made a wild dash for the barrel. Jim, not a hundred feet away, snapped a shot at him. Bonsell tripped, swiveled his head, saw Jim, and then rose to his feet.

This time he moved, moved toward Jim. He would face the inevitable. He walked slowly, and Jim saw him raise one gun and lower it as if he were throwing it, using it as a club. At the finish of its sweep, it exploded, and dust geysered in front of Jim.

Jim raised his gun slowly, tilted it toward the sky, then brought it down almost as slowly. Bonsell's second shot plucked at his sleeve, and still his gun came lower. When the black bulk of Bonsell's body blotted out the sights, Jim fired. He saw Bonsell stop, heard him grunt.

And then, in a wild surge of elation, he let go, both guns bucking into his palms, the wild sting of powder smoke in his nose, feet planted wide to meet anything Bonsell could throw at him.

He saw Bonsell's body jerk as though he were on strings as each slug caught him and jarred him.

And then his guns were empty. He waited, guns lowered. Bonsell took one lagging step toward him, stubborn and rawhide-tough to the end, then sighed mightily and fell. He was dead before he hit the ground.

Slowly Jim walked up to him. Scoville and Ben came running. The fire was brighter now, since the barrel had caught fire.

Jim knelt and turned Bonsell over. Reaching in his coat pocket, he drew out the charter. He looked at it and raised his eyes to Scoville.

There was a look of wild expectancy in Scoville's eyes. Jim could read it. It was as if Scoville had said, "There's the charter, Jim. It's yours, with nobody looking. Pick it up and run."

And then Jim said, in a weary voice, "It won't work, Phil. I couldn't do it. Mary couldn't take it."

The light in Scoville's eyes died, and he nodded. "That's right."

Ben lifted his head and listened and then said rapidly, "Jim, they're comin'! You better run!"

Jim only shook his head.

Scoville said quietly, pointing to Bonsell, "There's the only man that could have told the truth, Jim, about that squatter raid. And he's dead."

Jim only shook his head again, his gray eyes thoughtful and at peace.

"No, I'll give up, Phil. I've played my cards out—clean out."

Haynes and Cope and two other men came through the archway. Cope was running, his crutch winking in the light like the spokes of a wagon wheel.

When Haynes saw Jim Wade, he stopped, stared for the tenth part of a second, then made a grab for his gun.

Cope's crutch whipped across his wrist, pinning it to his gun butt.

"He's give up, you damn fool. Now watch what you're about."

Haynes drew his gun more carefully now. He covered Jim, and disarmed him, and then Ben. Afterward, he looked down at Bonsell.

"Now what's this about?" he asked harshly.

"There's your third bank robber," Jim said quietly. "And here's what he stole." He tendered Haynes the charter and other papers.

"What are they?"

"The charter to the Ulibarri grant," Jim murmured. "He stole them from Harvey Buckner's box, intending to sell them to Mary Buckner."

"Hah!" Haynes said, and raised his glance to Jim Wade. He couldn't keep the triumph from his eyes. "Looks like you played 'em so close to your chest, you couldn't even see 'em yourself, don't it, Wade?"

"Sort of looks like it," Jim agreed.

"You won't bust jail this time, my friend," Haynes said. Turning to the other men, he added, "Take aholt of his arms, you two. And Wade, if you make a break for it, I'll do just what I been wantin' to do ever since I first seen you. So help me, I'll shoot you in the back!"

Chapter Eighteen: STUBBORN

THE BANK WAS LIGHTED. Will-John Cruver lay stretched out on one of the desks, his legs hanging over the edge, breathing laboriously. Red foam flecked his beard, and his breath whistled sickeningly as it came and died. A circle of silent men watching him parted for Sheriff Haynes and Cope and Jim Wade.

Cruver's eyes shifted over to Jim Wade, and then he looked away.

"Can I try it?" Jim asked Haynes.

"Go ahead."

Jim stepped up to Cruver. "Will-John, I got Bonsell."

"Good," Cruver murmured.

Jim wondered what was keeping the man alive. It was nothing but his great fighting heart, his toughness.

"Goin' to pull through, Will-John?" Jim asked softly.

"Hunh-unh. This is it. I know."

"Want to talk?" Jim asked.

Cruver looked slowly at him. "What about?"

"Jim Buckner's murder," Jim answered. "Only your word stands between Mary Buckner and the Ulibarri grant, Will-John. And that girl never harmed a soul. Will you talk?"

Cruver whispered, "If I can."

"Then tell Haynes you and Donaldson, Boyd, Harmony, and Slocum killed him."

"Reed, too. We all killed him. We were scared."

"Where's he buried?"

Cruver only shook his head, as if he wouldn't answer. And then, seeming to change his mind, he murmured, "Above the spring on Mako Donaldson's place. That's what haunted Mako all these years."

Jim reached out and took Cruver's hand and squeezed it. Cruver smiled then, his great beard parting.

"You're a bucko boy, Jim," he whispered. "Some other time, some other place, we'd have made a pair." His eyes closed. "Too late," he murmured. "Too late."

He was quiet then. Nobody seemed to realize that he was dead, for Jim asked him a question. Cruver looked as if he was thinking about it, trying to answer. But there was no answer.

Jim looked up and said to Haynes, "That satisfy you, Haynes? James Buckner, the real heir to the grant, was killed by these men. And Mary Buckner is the rightful heir now."

"Mebbe," Haynes said. "It don't change what you done, though."

"No," Jim agreed quietly.

Haynes turned his attention to Warren, who was laid out on the floor. "Now, why was he in on this? And who is he? What's his real name?"

Nobody could answer that. Haynes went over and searched the man. There were papers in his coat pocket, some letters, and Haynes pocketed these, then turned to Jim and Cope.

"Well, it's jail for you, Wade."

They filed over to the office, the crowd growing behind them. Jim Wade's crime had been replaced by so many others that the townspeople did not seem hostile.

Mary Buckner was waiting in the sheriff's office. She took one look at Jim, shifted her glance to Cope, and then said in a dead voice, "You're holding Jim, Sheriff?"

"I am," Haynes said.

Mary looked at Jim. "What happened, Jim?"

"Bonsell broke into the bank with Cruver and Warren. He killed Warren, shot Cruver, and took the charter. We caught him down at the stable." He said faintly, "Cruver talked, Mary. He admitted the murder of your father."

"But I don't care!" Mary cried. She turned to Haynes. "You can't hold him, Sheriff! You can't! He's innocent!"

Haynes only shook his head and turned to the people crowding the office. "Clear out of here!" he said harshly. "Cope, you stay. I want Ben Beauchamp brought in here, too. The rest of you clear out."

They all cleared out except Scoville. To Scoville, the sheriff said, "You too, mister."

"I'll stick," Scoville said.

"And I say you'll get out!"

"Sheriff," Scoville drawled, "I got a gun on me. God knows I'd like to shoot you. Just say that again and I will.

Just give me a chance."

While he was talking, Lily Beauchamp slipped in through the door and closed it after her. Cope said to Haynes, "Sit down, Link. These people all belong here. Sit down here long enough to listen to the whole story."

Haynes sat on the desk, Mary in his chair, and Lily on the bench. The others listened while Cope talked. He talked first about Mary Buckner, bringing it up to the time Jim stepped in as the Excelsior foreman. Then he switched to Jim. He told of Bonsell's plan to saddle the burden of driving the squatters out on Jim's shoulders. The success of the scheme, Haynes had already seen. Then he told of what Jim had done since the jail break, how he had tried to avoid all this bloodshed.

Haynes listened carefully. When Cope was finished, Haynes said, "There's only one thing in that whole story that interests me as a sheriff, Cope."

"What's that?"

"You broke a prisoner out of jail and hid him. That's a crime."

To Ben Beauchamp, he said, "I don't want you. You can go any time." And then he settled back against the wall, his face smug and implacable.

Cope was speechless. That a man couldn't see what was plain as day, Cope couldn't understand. He wasn't angry; he was beyond that.

"Then you'll prosecute Jim?" he stammered.

"Unless somebody can prove that he didn't do it."

"But they're all dead! Except that outfit of gun fighters! And they're scattered to the four winds!" Cope protested.

"That's about it," Haynes said.

Jim looked over at Mary and then said, "Let that work itself out, Cope." To Haynes he said, "That charter. It belongs to Mary Buckner. Since you don't have to use it for evidence, will you give it to her?"

Haynes shook his head stubbornly. "No. It belongs to Harvey Buckner."

"But he stole it from Mary!"

"So you say. Can you prove it?"

Patiently, Jim went back over the old story. Haynes had heard it once, and he didn't appear interested. He toyed with a pen on the desk, listening idly to Jim's words. Then, while Jim talked, he shuffled through the pile of papers he had taken from Warren's pocket and which were lying on the desk. One caught his attention, simply because it was addressed to James Buckner, not to Ray Warren. Curiosity whetted, he ignored Jim's talk and drew the letter from its envelope. Jim, seeing what a hopeless thing he was trying to do, fell silent. Haynes didn't even notice the silence, for he was reading. And as he read, his eyes narrowed, and he licked his lips. When he finished, he turned back and read it through again.

Then he looked up at Jim Wade and said, "Well, I'll be damned."

"What?"

"This here is a letter from Max Bonsell addressed to Jim Buckner. What's it doin' on Warren?"

Nobody could answer that.

"It says," Haynes said slowly, "that the squatters is mostly driven off the Excelsior. Thirteen of 'em were killed. It also says that Bonsell's plan to frame Jim Wade with their murders worked right smart. It says that I'd got Wade in jail, but he broke loose."

With a growl, Cope grabbed the letter from the sheriff's hands and read through it. A slow grin broke over his face and he looked up at Haynes.

"Well, Sheriff, who's lyin' now?"

Haynes said sheepishly, "It looks like you was right about it, Wade."

"And I'm right about the charter," Jim said quickly.

He didn't see Mary's long sigh of relief, didn't see her covertly dab at her eyes. All Mary could understand of this was that Jim Wade, forgetful of himself, was trying desperately to convince Sheriff Haynes that she was the true heir to the Ulibarri acres.

Sheriff Haynes said, perhaps out of injured pride, "Maybe."

"Let's see that charter," Jim asked.

Sheriff Haynes unfolded the oilcloth. Inside, there was a limp paper folded three ways and yellow from age. Gently, Jim laid it flat on the desk, and they gathered round to look at it. It was written in the delicate, spidery hand of a court secretary, in ink old and faded. At the bottom was the Spanish emperor's signature, below it the heavy wax seal of the royal arms.

Jim searched for anything about it that would help, but there was nothing. The Ulibarri mentioned was lost in the dim pages of history, and standing here tonight was a girl in whose veins ran his blood.

"Look familiar?" he asked Mary quietly.

Mary nodded. "Yes, even the wrapper is the same."

"The oilcloth, you mean?"

Mary nodded. "I was so afraid I would hurt it. It seemed fragile, almost like dust. I had to protect it, and I thought the oilcloth would help."

Jim picked up the oilcloth. It was an ample square, its creases cracked away. Looking at its shiny side, Jim noticed a watermark on it, a pinkish stain which made a vague pattern of a fleur-de-lis.

"Where did you keep the charter, Mary?" he asked idly.

"In my trunk."

"Always?"

"When I was in Wyoming, yes. There wasn't a bank in the town."

Jim regarded the oilcloth with a frown. "Was it in your

trunk when it was stolen?"

"Yes."

"And you've still got the trunk?"

"It's over in my hotel now."

Jim raised his glance to Haynes. "What have we got to prove here, Haynes? That Mary is entitled to the charter?"

"Maybe she is," Haynes said. "Only Harvey Buckner had it. It's my duty to return it to his heirs. If you want it, you got to sue for it."

"But you don't believe it was stolen?"

"Might have been. I got to have proof."

"And if it was stolen, you'll return it to her?"

Haynes paused a moment, impressed by the importance of his decision. "Yes, I reckon I would."

Jim picked up the oilcloth and said, "Come along."

"Where?" Haynes asked.

"With me. You, too, Mary."

All of them filed over to the hotel, where Mary got her key. They went up to Mary's room, and Jim lighted the lamp.

"Where's your trunk, Mary?" he asked.

She pointed under the table. Jim got down on his knees, hauled it out, and lifted its contents onto a chair. He was smiling as he turned his glance up to Mary, then shifted it to Haynes.

"Come here Haynes. See the design on the paper that trunk is lined with? All right. See the design on this corner of the oilcloth? Now take a look at the bottom of that trunk. You'll see a stain, a water stain. That trunk sat out on some depot platform in the rain and it got soaked. The water seeped through the bottom, and the design came off on the oilcloth. They're the same."

He rose and watched Haynes poke around in the trunk. Then the sheriff rose.

"What more proof do you need, Haynes, that Mary Buckner once had that charter in that trunk? And if she hasn't got it now and Buckner has, don't that prove it was stolen?"

Cope swore softly, looking at Haynes. They were all looking at the sheriff. The evidence was conclusive. And while Sheriff Haynes was a stubborn man, he was also an honest one. He had admitted one error tonight; he wasn't afraid to admit another.

"It looks like the charter is hers," he announced quietly.

Cope let out a whoop of joy that might have come from a thirteen-year-old. He hugged Mary to him, patting her back, while she smiled over at Jim.

Sheriff Haynes scratched his head. "Well, it looks like I ain't got any business with you folks at all," he said. "Only Cope." He looked long at Cope. "Jack, you got a pretty record in this man's town. If I've said anything agin you, it was in anger." He put out his hand. "You're still the best man we got. And if you want to break my jail again, you're welcome to it."

He smiled broadly and went to the door. "Good night, folks," he murmured, and stepped out.

There were Scoville and Lily together, and there was Ben, clear-eyed and erect, holding Lily's other hand. And there was Cope next to Mary, and Jim next to her.

They all looked at each other, and it was Mary who said quietly, "And this is the end."

"Not quite," Scoville said, smiling. "Me and Lily aim to get married."

Lily looked over at Jim, and much lay in that glance. There was a secret between them, a conversation that Lily had once had with Jim at the jail window. She had meant it when she said it, maybe meant it now. Only this was her man. He was fine and brave and honest, and he'd be good to her. That's what Lily's eyes were trying to say. And Jim

Wade only smiled and nodded imperceptibly, then shook their hands.

Afterward, when Scoville and Lily and Ben and Cope had gone, Jim talked with Mary for a long hour until dawn began to light the east.

When he rose, a tall shape in that light, he took his hat and fumbled with it. How could a man say good-by?

"Where is it now, Jim?"

"Texas, I reckon. And you?"

"Here. Where I belong."

Jim looked long at her, so lovely and desirable and frail. Mary saw that look. She said quietly, "Why don't you say it, Jim?"

"What?"

"What you're thinking."

Jim said quietly, "All right, I will. I never saw a more beautiful girl than you, Mary. I love you so much that I'll never get you out of my blood." He paused. "There. That's what I was thinking, Mary."

"And I love you the same way, Jim," Mary murmured.

Jim dropped his hat. For one split second, he stood there, then moved toward her.

She was in his arms and she said quietly, "Oh, Jim, Jim, haven't you seen it? Couldn't you read it in my face, my eyes, for a long, long time?"

"Quiet, girl," Jim ordered, speaking into her hair, her body close to his. "I don't want to wake up."